Miss Frost Says I Do
and Spider Too

A Nocturne Falls Mystery

Jayne Frost, book seven

KRISTEN PAINTER

MISS FROST SAYS I DO
A Nocturne Falls Mystery
Jayne Frost, Book Seven

Copyright © 2019 Kristen Painter

ISBN: 978-1-941695-51-7

Published in the United States of America.

Welcome to Nocturne Falls — the town that celebrates Halloween 365 days a year.

Jayne Frost is a lot of things. Winter elf, Jack Frost's daughter, Santa Claus's niece, heir to the Winter Throne and soon to be newlywed.

Now that she and fiancé Sinclair (and their cats, Spider and Sugar) have moved back to the North Pole, they're firmly entrenched in planning their wedding. With Jayne's royal heritage, it's a major undertaking.

And while Jayne is trying to organize the myriad details, Sinclair is taking the necessary classes to learn how to be a royal and adjust to his impending new life as Prince Consort. But with too much assistance from her well-meaning mother and aunt, Jayne quickly gets overwhelmed.

Sinclair suggests calling a friend to help, the ever-resourceful Birdie Caruthers. Jayne does, and Birdie is thrilled to pitch in. Not long after she arrives, however, the trio discovers the most terrible thing in the wedding carriage.

Will this dreadful discovery derail the wedding? Or can they solve the problem in time to make it to the altar unscathed? Make no bones about it, this is some serious trouble.

Somewhere, somehow, in the communication process between me, my mother, my aunt, and LeRoy Bonfitte, the royal couturier who was my wedding dress designer, things had gone into a hard, sideways slide.

I took another look in the mirror as best I could. *Sideways* might be a touch too kind. Completely downhill at breakneck speed was probably more appropriate.

Not that I could really see myself in the mirror with the way the dress engulfed me. There was just so much of it. So much lace, so much tulle, so much ribbon, so much satin and beading and rhinestones and pearls and flowers and *no*.

I tried to get a breath of air that didn't taste like a wedding disaster and failed. Eyes closed for a moment, I did my best not to lose my cool entirely.

If I'd been alone, the whole situation would have been a lot easier.

But beyond the storm of satin swirling around me, my mother and aunt eagerly awaited my reaction. I had to tread carefully, but at the same time, how much could I sugarcoat this truth and still be true to myself? This was my wedding after all, and this dress was nothing like the picture in my head. Or what I thought I'd discussed with LeRoy. I took another breath. "This dress is..."

"Divine?" My aunt's voice piped up.

I growled softly. "More like disastrous."

"Jayne!" I couldn't see my mother past the enormous bow or rose or whatever was on my shoulder, but I obviously knew her voice.

"Well, it is." I tried to turn to see her, but the yards of fabric swamping me made that impossible. This dress defied description. It was as if every wedding dress in the history of wedding dresses had been sewn together into one monstrous Frankendress. Forget Bridezilla, this was Gownzilla.

Something inside me snapped. "I am not wearing this down the aisle. Literally. Because that would be impossible. I can't walk more than a few steps in this thing without getting tripped."

I could, however, probably crouch down inside it and disappear. The idea held more merit with each passing moment.

"Jayne, honey, it's a wedding dress. It's supposed to be over-the-top," Aunt Martha chimed in. "And you love over-the-top." The tone of her voice told me she was probably wringing her hands.

"It's true. I am all about over-the-top. But this left the top behind fifteen yards of fabric ago." I grabbed hold of the shoulder flounces and flattened them so I could see my family. Then I looked them squarely in the eyes. "This is *not* the dress I ordered."

Just then, LeRoy Bonfitte walked into the grand salon. His assistant, Charlotte, must have told him I was dressed in his creation and standing before the three-paneled mirror meant to show me just how amazing I looked.

As if.

"Princess Jayne." He bowed with a flourish and a smile. "How marvelous to see you. And how marvelous you look. You are happy, no?"

I smiled in an attempt to soften my response, because I knew he wasn't solely responsible for this explosion of all things bridal. Also, he was a wonderful man and a talented designer, and I liked and needed him very much. "No, I'm afraid not."

His face fell. "What's wrong?"

"Well, to start with, LeRoy, this isn't the dress we talked about." The dress we'd talked about had probably been eaten by the dress I was wearing. "Secondly, does this dress really look like me?"

He shot a quick glance at my mother and aunt, confirming my suspicions that they'd influenced him. But then, I already knew that based on all the extras that had been added to the gown.

I let go of one of the bows to hold my hand up. "I don't need an explanation. I just want something more like what we originally talked about. I don't mind your creative interpretation of that, so long as you think it will suit me. I trust *you*."

He nodded solemnly. "Yes, Your Highness."

He left, head down, brow furrowed, and I knew he was blaming himself for letting my mom and aunt sway him. I felt awful.

I put a hand to my head and sighed. "This wedding is going to kill me. I need to change out of this monstrosity and go apologize, then I'm going to disappear into a vat of sugar until I no longer feel like breaking something."

My aunt and my mother just stared at me with rounded eyes and slightly horrified expressions.

My mother finally found her voice. "I think that's a marvelous idea. You need to decompress. And I can talk to LeRoy for you." She cleared her throat. "After all, it's because of my and Martha's suggestions that your dress looks the way it does, I'm afraid."

"I know." I frowned at them. "I saw the way he looked at you. And I know you both mean well, but in all honesty, I'm kind of reaching a breaking point. This wedding is supposed to be a joyous day filled with love and happiness."

Aunt Martha nodded. "Yes, absolutely."

"But you know what I'm thinking about instead of a magical wedding day?" I leaned forward as far as the dress would allow and stressed the one word I knew would put fear into them. "*Eloping.*"

My mother and Aunt Martha both pulled back, cringing at the word.

"Please don't do that," my mother whispered.

I just shrugged, letting the whole thing play out even though the big wedding was an inevitability. "Right now, it's fifty-fifty."

Aunt Martha grabbed my mother's arm. "We'll go talk to LeRoy right now. We'll make everything right, you'll see."

"That's a start."

They speed-walked off to find him.

But all I could think was, *Mission accomplished.* The fear of my eloping should keep them on the straight and narrow. At least for today.

That didn't change the fact that I really was on the verge of losing it. There was so much going on I couldn't keep it straight, so many decisions to make, and all of it falling on my shoulders. Clearly, it had to be that way, because if I let my mom and aunt do it, I was going to end up with some kind of bridal nightmare.

And Sinclair, since he wasn't royal or officially Prince Consort yet, could only help so much. Some things required my official seal of approval.

On top of all that, everything had to be approved by the Royal Etiquette Committee. I'd dealt with them before in some very minor ways, but with this wedding, it felt like they were sitting on my shoulder, shaking their heads at everything I did.

Being a princess had all kinds of strings attached. Not being able to have the final say on your wedding planning was one of them. Although, if they said no to something Sin and I really wanted, I was prepared to fight them.

Look, I got that my wedding to Sinclair wasn't just two people getting hitched. It was the future of the North Pole happening in real time. A celebration of Winter and Christmas royalty. It was also the event of the century. I wasn't kidding. My parents had one child, one heir to the Winter Throne. Me.

So yeah, this was a major deal.

I understood every bit of that. Understood the significance of the marriage in the scheme of North Pole history and royal succession and so forth and so on. But at the moment, I was just a girl trying to marry the guy she loved. And I was just about over all the fuss and bother that being royal entailed.

Not to mention, Sin and I were still working through the details of the renovation on the apartment that would be our home when this wedding was done with. That was a major undertaking in itself.

Alone in the grand salon, I ducked down, found the floor and tunneled out of the dress. When I was free of it, I got to my feet, lifted my chin, and walked back to the dressing room in my bra and underwear with as much dignity as possible.

What I needed was to see my guy and decompress a little, maybe hang out with just him and our cats, Spider and Sugar, but I wasn't sure that could happen anytime soon. He was immersed in his own hectic schedule of classes, learning all kinds of things he'd need to know as Prince Consort. Things like our royal history, royal etiquette, how to address people, what his role would be once I became queen, and what charities there were for him to work with as Prince Consort. He'd also be hiring his new staff and having meetings with them about what he expected, what his needs would be, and probably a thousand other things that were already part of my daily life.

Everything I'd grown up with and come to think of as just part of life was now being added to his.

There was a good chance he was as overwhelmed as I was. That concerned me. I didn't need my groom stressed out as much as I was. One of us had to stay sane.

I put my jeans, sweater, and boots back on and was about to exit the dressing room just as my phone chimed. Since the tech teams had installed the new landlines that Ingvar, the new IT team leader had designed, local communication had vastly improved.

Unless you didn't like people being able to reach you. In that case, things had taken a turn for the worse.

Or, in the case of my aunt and mother, who'd discovered all the wedding boards on Pinterest, things had gotten very...Pinteresty. Much to my detriment.

I'd stopped trying to explain to both of them that in order for me to see something on Pinterest that they liked, they didn't need to print out and messenger it to me, but the concept of emailing me a link never seemed to take hold.

I checked the screen and saw a reminder that I was due at the Royal Transportation Division in thirty minutes to review the Crystal Carriage that would carry me from the palace, through the streets of the North Pole, then to the town square where an ice cathedral specifically constructed for the wedding would host the actual ceremony.

After we said our vows, the carriage would then take Sin and me through the streets again and eventually return us to the palace for the reception. The ride through the city would be our first official duty as husband and wife. The first time for the citizens to see us as such. The carriage alone was something to behold, but with us inside it? Quite the spectacle. I couldn't imagine the crowds.

The carriage was used for three main royal events—funerals, naming ceremonies, and weddings. None of those things had happened in a long, long time.

My guess was that the thing had a solid layer of dust or frost on it, depending on how well maintained the transportation hangar was.

But today, I didn't care if it was buried under fifty feet of polar bear poop. I'd had my fill of wedding planning and all things wedding related.

I needed Sin, some downtime, hefty quantities of sugar, and a chatty little black cat on my lap.

I sent a quick text to the Transportation Division to tell them today's visit was off, and I would reschedule at my earliest convenience. It had been years since I'd seen the carriage in person, but it wasn't a pressing issue.

Next I texted Sin. *Where are you and what are you doing?*

While I waited for him to answer, I grabbed my purse and headed for the crawler I'd driven here. As soon as I was behind the wheel, Sin's reply came through.

Meeting with the security team about the wedding, then supposed to go to a lesson on proper attire for official daytime functions.

I cringed on his behalf. *But you don't really want to do that, do you?*

Not even remotely a little bit. What's up?

I need a break that includes you and some sugar. And no wedding talk.

I'm in. Where?

I gave that a moment of thought. As much as I wanted to see the cats, going back to the palace would make us too easy to find. I wasn't ready to be tracked down just yet. *How about a movie? We can be alone in the royal box. I don't even care what's showing.*

Me either. Pick me up at the south exit in ten?

I smiled big. *On my way.*

It actually took me nine minutes, and Sin didn't make it out for two more after that, but then we were headed to the theater, and the wedding stuff was temporarily behind us.

He sighed as he sat back. "It's a good thing I love you."

"I know." I shook my head. "It's a lot, isn't it?"

"It is. But I knew what I was getting into. At least I thought I did. This might be more than my doughnut maker's brain can take in."

"No way. You're one of the smartest men I know." I did my best to keep things positive. "But I get it. It's overwhelming at the moment. Someday this will all be old hat."

"I'm sure, but right now, it's making my head

throb. I don't know how you do it. Except that you were born into it."

"I know," I repeated. "I'm sorry."

He smiled at me. "Don't apologize. It's all worth it to marry you. But let's just say your timing on this little escape was perfect."

"I needed it, too, trust me."

"Dare I ask why?"

"I'll just say dress disaster and leave it at that."

He frowned. "I thought you had a designated designer."

"I do, and he's wonderful, but my mother and Aunt Martha got a little too involved in the process, and it ended up looking more like an avalanche of satin than something anyone would want to wear down the aisle. It's not LeRoy's fault. How do you say no to the queen and Mrs. Kringle? But it's all going to be fixed. I just had enough for the day, that's all."

"I understand." He deftly changed the subject. "What's showing?"

"I'm not sure, actually. I think there's a rom-com and an action flick to pick from."

"Well, I'm up for anything."

"Good." I pulled into the theater's parking lot, found a space, and turned off the crawler's engine. The marquee announced what was playing.

I read the movie titles out loud. "*Pirates of the Pacific*. That's that one with JLo and The Rock as pirates competing to find the treasure before the other one, but then they end up falling in love and joining forces against their mutual archnemesis."

Sin shrugged. "Sounds like mindless fun."

"It does. Or there's something called *Three by Night*. I'm not sure what that one is."

"I just saw the trailer for that. It's Simon Pegg, Pierce Brosnan, and Kate Winslet as a team of vampire agents trying to keep the world from finding out vampires are real after the fourth member of their team, Kevin Hart, accidentally outs himself on a Facebook Live video."

I laughed. "Too late. We already know vampires are real."

Sin grinned. "Well, some of us do. Which one do you want to see?"

"I don't care. Whichever one starts next is fine with me."

"Then that's what we'll see."

Turned out to be *Three by Night*. We—meaning me—loaded up on kettle corn, Junior Mints, Raisinets, Swedish Fish, and Sno-Caps. Plus, a large cherry slush. Sin got nachos and a Coke. He also helped me carry everything up to the royal box, where we settled into the plush recliners and disappeared into the movie for an hour and forty-five minutes.

It was blissful. But when the movie ended, reality came crashing back. The credits rolled on by, but I stayed in my chair.

Sin looked over. "Are you okay?"

I shook my head, on the verge of tears for no reason I could name. "That was fun, but I am still incredibly stressed, and I hate it."

"I hate it too. So let's elope. We can get a flight to Vegas and be married tomorrow."

I smiled at him, the urge to cry wiped away by how understanding he was. "I would love that, but it would cause more problems than I want to think about."

"I had a feeling." He brushed a strand of hair off my cheek. "Babe, you're never going to make it through this without some help. We have a contractor for the apartment renovation. Why don't you hire a wedding planner to help with the rest?"

I groaned. "Royals don't do that. For one thing, it would mean an outside influence on a royal wedding, which would be frowned on big-time. For another, it's not tradition. I mean, we already have people for everything, so it's supposed to be easy, but..." I shook my head. "It's so not."

Sin pondered that a moment. "What if you didn't *exactly* hire a wedding planner, but you just happened to bring a friend in who just happened to be really good at organizing this kind of stuff?"

I squinted at him, amused by what he was suggesting. "You're not even officially a royal yet, and already you're figuring out ways around the system? You're going to do just fine in the North

13

Pole. Do you have someone in mind? Because it sure seems like you do."

He grinned, then shrugged a little. "There's only one person I can think of who could wrangle this wedding business into order. I'm sure she'd be happy to leave Nocturne Falls for a trip to the NP if you asked. But I have a feeling you already know who I'm talking about."

At the same time, the same name came out of both our mouths.

"Birdie Caruthers."

I owed Juniper, the elf who'd taken over for me as manager at the toy shop in Nocturne Falls, for getting Birdie on the snow globe so quickly. I'd have to send Juni a pound of Aunt Martha's famous eggnog fudge as a thank-you. That was always well received, whatever the occasion.

Birdie, being the awesome and amazing person she was, needed no convincing to make the trip to the North Pole.

When her squealing subsided, I was still laughing. My smile was making my cheeks hurt. "You're sure they can spare you at the station? Can you even get the time off?"

She waved the question away like I was silly for asking. "Oh, honey, for one thing, I've been training a girl to take over for me while I'm up there for the wedding, so I already have someone to fill in. This'll be a good chance for her to get stuck in. Secondly, I have so much vacation time squirreled away that this trip is going to make me money. Now, how do I get there?"

I gave her the rundown on getting a flight to Anchorage, then where to find the portal that would lead her to the NP. All with the promise that I'd have transportation waiting. Which I would. I just had to put in a request for one of the guys from the vehicle pool.

"That sounds great. I guess I'll see you in two days, unless there's some issue getting a flight, which I don't think there will be. How many first class seats from Atlanta to Anchorage do you think they sell, anyway?" She laughed, cheeks rosy with happiness. "This is going to be a blast."

"I'm so glad you think so."

"My dear, planning a wedding is no different than running this station. You'll see. You just let Birdie take care of everything."

"That's my intention. See you soon. And thank you."

She winked. "You betcha."

We hung up our respective globes, and for the first time in a long time, I let out a sigh of relief. Birdie was going to be exactly the help I needed. I'd get her a room in the palace close to mine. Which meant I needed to let Ezreal know so he could take care of the arrangements.

As the new palace steward, it was his job to

organize such things. Since he'd been promoted to the position from his former job as my father's office manager some months ago, he hadn't had any guests to deal with.

Birdie would be his first. I guessed that's what you'd call a baptism by fire. Not that Birdie was difficult. Not in any way, shape, or form. But she was a genuine character and definitely had her own opinions about things. I thought Ezreal would enjoy her.

And I had no doubt that she would enjoy Ezreal. The half winter elf, half ice troll was the kind of guy Birdie would probably refer to as eye candy. Although, she was seriously dating Jack Van Zant, so I didn't think she'd do more than flirt a little.

Either way, it would be interesting to see her in action in the North Pole. I wasn't sure how she'd handle this level of cold. She was a werewolf, so the chill shouldn't bother her too much, but then again, she was a Georgia girl and used to the heat.

Well, the palace had a vast supply of warm clothing for any guest who hadn't packed properly.

Birdie would be fine. I'd see to that personally.

For the next two days, Sin and I played hooky from wedding-planning duties. Any appointment that came up, we canceled with an excuse. We also made ourselves scarce, spending time holed up in one of our apartments (which were across the hall from each other), bingeing some TV series we were behind on, playing with the cats until they were tired of all their toys, or sneaking out and taking long drives in the crawler to the polar forest just to admire the beauty and stillness of the place.

One night, when we were supposed to be auditioning quartets to play at the ceremony, we canceled and took an evening drive to see the northern lights play across the sky. We brought a picnic basket full of goodies from the kitchen and sat for hours, watching the twisting ribbons of color brighten the heavens.

We both knew we were shirking our responsibilities, but those two days of downtime were magical. We were reminded of why we fell in love, and the time off was like a giant recharge of our collective batteries. Having Birdie on the way helped too. But the break from the wedding madness couldn't have come at a better time.

Instead of sending a driver for Birdie, Sin and I picked her up in a crawler. Not only because she deserved the personal touch and I was eager to see her, but because Sin and I had arranged a little surprise for her.

I threw my arms open wide when she came through the Anchorage portal at the travel station on the outskirts of town. "Birdie!"

Her eyes lit up when she saw me. "Hi, Princess." She hugged me right back.

Sin collected her luggage. One bag and a carry-on. "Is this all?"

She nodded as she released me. "What did you expect? I'm not Zsa Zsa Gabor. Not that you probably have any idea who that is."

Sin gave her a look. "Hey, I've seen *Green Acres*."

I laughed. "Eva Gabor was in *Green Acres*."

"Well, I'm not her either," Birdie said.

"No, you're not a Gabor sister, but you are a snappy dresser. I expected you'd have more luggage too."

She grinned. "I plan on doing a little shopping while I'm here. I don't have many winter clothes, so I just brought the basics and figured I'd pick up whatever else I needed. You do have shopping up here, don't you?"

"Do we? Oh, you just wait." I was so thrilled to have her here. "Welcome to the North Pole, Birdie. Come on, we're going to give you a little tour on the way to the palace."

I let her sit up front with Sin, then I narrated all the important sights and locations as we passed them.

She was enthralled, which I loved, because it was important to me that she liked my kingdom. What could I say? The role of future ruler was really settling on me. And I loved this place, even more so now that I had Sin here with me.

In that moment, I could've burst with the love

and pride I felt for my home and my life and the man I was going to share it with. The wedding planning was a giant pain in the backside, but Birdie was here, and we would get through this.

Before I could blink, Sin and I would be married and living our day-to-day life. I needed to find a way to appreciate all the moments that were coming up, because they weren't going to be repeated again.

The thought calmed me and filled me with a new resolve for what lay before us.

Birdie shook her head as we passed the town square. "This place is magical. I mean, I know it's literally magical, but it's like a Christmas dream come true. You two are so lucky to live here."

I smiled and put a hand on Sin's shoulder. "We are."

Sin glanced back, eyes gleaming with the same kind of pride I felt. "We sure are. But we're really glad you came, Birdie. This wedding stuff is getting to Jayne." He shook his head. "I can't have my baby stressed out like this."

Birdie looked at me. "Bad, huh?"

I sighed. "It is. I'm sad to say that nowhere in my years of training to take the crown did I prepared for the chaos of a royal wedding. And it goes without saying that I love my mother and my aunt beyond words, but they both have big visions of what this wedding should look like, and I don't know how to tell them that their ideas don't jive with my ideas. I don't want to hurt their feelings. I know how excited about this wedding they are."

Birdie was nodding enthusiastically. "Honey, you just leave it to me. All they can see is how much they love you and want you to have every good thing possible. They just need an outside opinion to show them that sometimes less really is more. And letting the bride have her day her way means everyone's happy."

"Well, good luck." If she could actually achieve that, I'd make her an honorary citizen of the realm.

Sin turned the crawler away from the palace and toward our predetermined destination.

Birdie didn't miss a beat. She pointed. "Isn't that the palace over there?"

"It is," Sin answered. "But Jayne thought you might want to dive into the wedding business right away."

Birdie turned around so she could see me, and her face lit up. "Are we going cake tasting? Please say we're going cake tasting. I could go for something to eat."

I laughed. "No, not yet, but that is on the list of things we need to do. I think there's already an appointment set up too. But right now, there's something much more pressing."

"Oh?" She seemed riveted. I guess she really was cut out for this.

"I need to give my approval to the Crystal Carriage that will drive me, then the both of us as a married couple, through the streets. The approval is purely ceremonial. No royal in the history of the carriage's use has ever not approved it, but it still has to be done. I wanted Sin to come with me to see the carriage, then I thought you might get a kick out of it too. Is that all right? We're headed to one of the transportation buildings where it's stored."

"All right? It sounds wonderful. It's a very romantic piece of North Pole history, isn't it?"

"It is. My parents rode in it when they were married, and my grandparents before them and so on." I looked at Sin. "And someday, our children will ride in it with their spouses."

I could see him smile in the rearview mirror.

Birdie put her hand to her cheek. "You're making me misty." She dropped her hand. "But I'd still like cake. Just saying."

"There's cake at the palace, I promise. And it's an all-you-can-eat, twenty-four seven, situation."

She turned back around and sighed a happy sigh.

But when we pulled into the parking lot of the Transportation Division, I could tell she was a little underwhelmed. The simple metal buildings were enormous but didn't look like a whole lot. They were about as utilitarian as, well, any other government storage buildings might be.

I leaned in. "It gets better inside."

Her surprised expression told me she hadn't expected me to pick up on what she was thinking. "Oh, I'm sure, Princess."

We went into the third building on the left, where we were met by Tianna Silverleaf, head of the Royal Transportation Division.

She bowed. "Welcome, Your Highness, Consort Sinclair, and your guest. I am honored to show you the Crystal Carriage for your approval."

"Thank you, Tianna. This is Birdie Caruthers. She's our wedding advisor."

Tianna smiled and clutched a clipboard to her chest. "How lovely to meet you, Ms. Caruthers."

Birdie's entire being expanded slightly at her new title. "And you."

I gave Tianna a little nod. "We're ready when you are."

"Then let me lead the way."

She tapped a code into a keypad on a nearby door, then opened it and stood waiting for us to come through. "Welcome to Hangar Nine."

Stepping into Hangar Nine was hard to describe. Not the building itself. It was in all ways a typical vehicle storage facility with several sets of large garage doors, overhead mercury vapor lighting that cast a blue-white gleam on everything, and a polished concrete floor that was easy to clean and showed off what was kept there.

But the vehicles Hangar Nine held? That's where it got interesting.

Birdie's small gasp was testament to that. She pointed. "Is that…what I think it is?"

I nodded at the large antique red-and-gold sled closest to us. Its black leather seats were cracked and worn from age and its brass a little tarnished, but it was still a beautiful sight. "The very first one. Hasn't flown in centuries, but it probably still could."

Sinclair shook his head. "Wow. That is really something." He looked around. "How many sleighs are here?"

"All of them," Tianna answered. "When they're retired, they come to us for storage and preservation."

His brows furrowed as he looked at me. "Seems like there should be a dedicated museum for that. Don't you think?"

I shrugged. "I guess that's kind of what this is. Except it's not open to the public. Which is sad, when I think about it."

Tianna wrapped both arms around her clipboard. "We used to give tours to some of the school and charity groups, but that hasn't been for a long while now."

"That's a shame." Sinclair looked genuinely upset the tours weren't still happening.

"Why did they stop?" I asked.

Tianna seemed more than happy to answer.

"The superintendent of schools ended the program. That was before my time here, though. Maybe twenty-five years ago? But I don't know why."

"Let me guess," Sinclair said. "Budget concerns?"

I made a face. "Not in the NP. Our schools are top-notch. No expenses spared."

Birdie frowned. "Then why cancel the tours? I would think the children would love to see this part of their history."

I had no answer. "We can certainly ask my father or my uncle. They should know. But we should get to the reason we came." Especially since Birdie wanted cake. "The carriage."

"Of course." Tianna gestured toward the rear of the building. "Right this way."

We followed her past years of sleds, some original crawler replicas, a bicentennial biplane that my uncle had once driven in a parade, a few other ceremonial carriages, and a custom-made Harley-Davidson Fat Boy, designed especially for my uncle, until finally we came to the one and only Crystal Carriage.

It was shaped like an egg on its side, covered in irregular facets that made it seem part gem, part shards of ice. The bottom half was frosted, but then turned clear at the midpoint, allowing the riders inside to be visible, although we couldn't see inside right now because the carriage sat up on an ornate silver cage. That cage was supported by equally ornate silver wheels that were as tall as Sin. All of the silver bits were inset with more shards of gleaming North Pole crystal.

There was nothing else like the carriage in all the realm. Or anywhere, I'd venture to guess.

Tianna clicked a small remote attached to the top of her clipboard, and spotlights came on, making the carriage sparkle like an enormous jeweled brooch.

"Butter my biscuit," Birdie muttered. Her mouth remained open.

I had to admit, it was really something. So many years had passed since I'd seen it in person that even my recollection of it had dimmed. "You can say that again."

Sin ran a hand through his hair. "We're going to ride in that?"

Tianna nodded. "While it might not look like it has an opening, there are gull-wing-style panels on both sides that allow access." She smiled. "The lights show it off a bit, but when you see it in the sun—"

Birdie snorted. "In the sun, that thing will blind people."

I chuckled. "Winter elves are used to the flash of sun on ice and snow. Which is probably why we like sparkly things so much."

"And sugar," Birdie said. "It's also kind of sparkly and looks like snow."

"True." Boy, she really did have cake on the brain. "Maybe we can swing by one of the bakeries on the way back to the—"

Sin cleared his throat. "Before you two start a carb-forward shopping list, maybe we can finish what we came here to do?"

There was amusement in his eyes. I shook my head. "Such a taskmaster." I looked at Tianna. "I just need to sign off on the paperwork?"

"Sure, if you're done with your inspection."

I hadn't actually *inspected* the carriage. "I suppose I should have a look inside, see what kind of room is in there. The last time I rode in it, I was three months old and on my way to my naming ceremony. Can't say as I remember much."

Birdie leaned in. "Can I look inside too?"

"Sure. Sin, come with us. Might as well since we're all here." I glanced at Tianna. "How do we open the doors?"

"There's a lever set into the chassis on both sides, but the livery will take of that for you on your wedding day." She walked over and pulled the hidden lever.

With a little hiss, the door separated from the carriage and split at the midline, one side rising into the air. The bottom half lowered, opening into steps that descended from the silver cage the carriage rested in. They were embedded on the facing edge with more crystal.

"Very snazzy," Birdie said. "Would it be okay if I took a picture? It's not like I can post it to social media or anything. I heard there's no connection up here."

"There didn't used to be," I said. "But one of our engineers has been working on that. It's a lot better than it used to be. At least in town. Sending texts and making calls beyond the North Pole is still questionable, though. Long answer to say, yes, a picture would be fine as long as you don't share it."

Sin held his hand out. "Why don't you two go stand on the steps and I'll take it?"

"That would be wonderful. Thank you, Sinclair." Birdie handed her phone to him, then hustled over to the carriage.

I leaned up and kissed his cheek. "You're the best. Come join us when you're done so you can have a look too."

"I will." He held the phone up to frame the shot.

Birdie was standing very still on the third step, facing into the carriage. Her expression wasn't exactly one of wonder and delight. "Um, Princess?"

"On my way," I answered as I made my way over.

She looked over her shoulder. "Good. Because I think you're going to want to see this."

"See what?" I asked.

Birdie pointed into the carriage. "Not really a what so much as a whom. At least I think that applies."

"Huh?" I climbed onto the second step and peered past her only to suck in a sharp breath when I saw what she was pointing at. "Son of a nutcracker."

A skeleton. On the carriage floor.

Constable Larsen made it to the Transportation Division in record time, but that was probably due to the police station being on the same side of town.

As I finished telling her how we'd discovered the remains, she shook her head. "This is very unusual."

"I'll say." I didn't think a skeleton had ever been found before in the NP like this. Or ever that I could remember, anyway. "Are there any missing-persons reports that might give us a clue as to who this is?"

"Can't say without digging into those files, but it's where I'm going to start." She glanced toward the carriage. "Obviously, I'll have the ME do a thorough investigation of the remains as well."

"We have a medical examiner? I mean, obviously we have one. Who is it?"

"Dr. Charming. He should be here shortly. I

called him right after Tianna called me. I figured if there was a body, no sense in wasting time."

"I appreciate that." The constable had come a long way in the last year. Increasing her budget had given her not only some much-needed help in the form of more deputies, but a real confidence boost. We'd even had an addition built onto the station that contained three holding cells. Three might have been overkill, but it made a point. "Isn't he also a regular doctor?"

"Yes, but that's because as the ME he doesn't get much work." She shrugged. "The man's got to keep busy."

"I suppose that's true. Well, he's going to be busy now."

"He's got a PA to help in the office, so if you're worried about his doctoring getting in the way, it won't."

"I wasn't, but good to know." Okay, maybe I was thinking about the possibility that his other job might interfere, but Dr. Charming had a good reputation. I was sure he wasn't going to slack when there were royals involved. We tended to inspire people to do their best.

Two of her deputies were cataloging everything on the scene. Taking photos, talking to the four of us, and making sure to partition the area off with yellow crime-scene tape that had probably never been used. Frankly, I was surprised the department had any. But there was little chance of the area being disturbed. No one came into this hangar unless it was for some official reason.

That really made the tape unnecessary, but I imagined the deputies were excited about getting to use it.

One of the deputies, Givens, approached me. He was a gnarled, older man who probably would have been a tinker or builder if not for his decision to go into law enforcement. I nodded at him. "Deputy."

He gave a quick bow in return. "Princess. Quite the thing, eh?"

"I'll say."

"Hate to ask, but just wanted to double-check that your fingerprints are on file?"

"They are. Royal protocol. But I don't think Sinclair's had his done yet, and I know you won't find my guest's on file. Her name is Birdie Caruthers."

He nodded and made a note of that in his book. "They'll have to come by the station and—"

Constable Larsen interrupted him. "Givens, we can send someone to the palace to do prints."

I knew how Birdie would feel about that. She'd not only *want* to go down to the station, but she'd probably expect a tour too. "We don't need any exceptions made."

Sinclair joined us just then. "Exceptions to what?"

"Exceptions to…" I thought a second. "Standard operating procedures, I guess. You and Birdie will have to go down to the station and be fingerprinted."

At the sound of her name, Birdie headed in our direction.

He shrugged. "I have to do it anyway, right?"

"Yes, but that would have been done at the palace."

The constable nodded vigorously. "Like the princess said, getting your prints is just standard procedure."

"So you can eliminate our prints from any others you find," Birdie added as she caught the last bit. "I know the drill."

I grinned. "Birdie works at the Nocturne Falls Sheriff's Department. She's the receptionist and all-around information center of that place. Plus, her nephew is the sheriff, so she's pretty versed in law enforcement."

Birdie beamed. Her pride in her nephew, Hank Merrow, was no small thing.

The constable's brows went up. "Is that so? Well, that's good to know. In case we need to deputize you for additional help."

I was sure Larsen was just being nice, since she had no idea what Birdie was capable of, but I couldn't think of a better candidate for deputizing than Birdie.

"You just let me know." Birdie leaned in to see the

constable's name on her badge better. "Constable Larsen. Happy to help."

The constable nodded. "I'll be sure to do that." She looked at me. "I'll keep you informed on what I find too."

"And Dr. Charming's discoveries as well," I added. "As I'm sure you understand, a skeleton in the carriage is rather concerning."

"Yes, absolutely. I'll be in touch." She went off to talk to her deputies.

Sin moved closer to Birdie and me. "Do you want to wait until the doctor gets here, or do you want to leave now?"

"We should go," Birdie said abruptly. Then she kind of caught herself. "If that's okay with you, Princess."

"Sure. I'm definitely ready to go. Is everything okay?"

Birdie tipped her head down and whispered, "Not here."

That could only mean Birdie had information she wanted to share with us alone, but I couldn't imagine what that might be. I waved at the constable. "Talk to you soon."

Then I gave Birdie and Sin a look. "Let's go."

Once we were back in the crawler with the doors shut, I said, "Spill it, Birdie. What didn't you want to say in there? And *why* didn't you want to say it in there?"

Birdie, in the front seat again, turned so she could see Sin and me. Her gaze held concern. "I know those people are your law enforcement, but that one deputy was setting off my alarms. But that might just be because he reminds me of the last tourist Hank arrested for drunk and disorderly." She shrugged. "Anyway, I wanted to keep what I found between us. Until you say differently, Princess."

"What you found?" I was sure my brows were nearly touching my hairline.

She reached into her coat pocket and pulled out a tiny scrap of fabric. "This. Does it look familiar?"

I took the postage stamp-size piece off her palm. "Looks like ivory silk with thin pearl and silver threads running through it. Very fancy. Definitely the kind of thing that someone riding in that carriage might wear. But I don't recognize it beyond that."

Even Sin seemed fascinated by it. "Couldn't you go back through royal photographs and see if it matches something worn by someone who would have been in the carriage in the past?"

Birdie nodded. "That's a great idea. And if they're not missing, then they might be the killer."

"First of all, that's kind of a leap. Secondly…" I glared nicely at both of them. "These are my relatives you're talking about, you know. I don't think any of them are capable of murder. Okay, maybe my father. Never mind, forget I said that. Thirdly, we have no idea what the cause of death is yet. Could be natural causes."

Sin tipped his head with obvious skepticism. "Sweetheart, who dies of natural causes in a carriage like that? Not to be indelicate, but there was no sign of decomposition. And wouldn't they have had to been naked? There were no clothes on the skeleton. Just bones."

"Right. Which would be weirder yet." I couldn't really think of any normal reasons for a person to be naked in the royal ceremonial carriage. Just really not-normal ones. "I'm just saying we don't have all the facts."

Birdie's smile was meant to be calming, I was sure of it. "No, we don't, so we shouldn't be jumping to conclusions. It's such a tiny scrap. It could have come from anywhere. There's more of a chance it's not related to the skeleton at all."

"Exactly." But there was something about her tone that said she was holding something back. I sighed. "Where did you find it?"

Birdie pursed her lips. "Under the skeleton's foot."

My mouth fell open. "You moved the skeleton? Isn't touching anything at a crime scene forbidden?"

"I didn't move the skeleton. I saw the fabric peeking out, and I grabbed it." She shrugged. "It seemed important."

Sin nodded. "If it was under the skeleton, I don't think we can rule it out as not being evidence."

I sat back. "I guess not." I frowned. "I can't believe anyone I'm related to could be involved in this."

Sin twisted around farther in the driver's seat. "I don't think they are. It's more likely that skeleton was put in the carriage to hide it. Nothing about the interior of that carriage looks like a murder scene. But just for the sake of conversation, who else might have ridden in the carriage besides one of your relatives?"

"I don't really know. But Tianna would be able to pull up the records on that." I sat up a little straighter. "Actually, Ezreal could access them a lot faster."

"Who's Ezreal?" Birdie asked.

"The palace steward," Sin answered. "And a really good guy."

I looked at Sin. "We need to get on top of this before any rumors start."

He faced forward and grabbed the wheel. "Hang on, ladies. We're about to see just how fast this thing can go."

Sin wasn't kidding about seeing how fast the crawler could go. He put the pedal down, and we made it to the palace faster than I thought possible. It was clear he enjoyed the drive, especially when his face lit up at the snow plumes the crawler sprayed out going around turns.

We practically skidded to a stop at the south entrance, which wasn't where I'd hoped to end up. I'd wanted to bring Birdie in through the front because it was the most impressive, but given the circumstances, I didn't think she minded.

Ezreal greeted us as we walked inside. "Welcome back, Princess, Consort. And a very special first-time welcome for our royal guest, Ms. Caruthers."

I didn't know how he knew we'd be arriving, but he was just good like that. A bellman with him carried a silver tray bearing three cups of steaming hot chocolate. With a little bow, the bellman offered us the drinks. We each took one.

"Hi, Ezreal. Thank you for the hot chocolate." I put my hand on Birdie's arm. "I'm pleased to introduce you to my friend, Birdie Caruthers. Birdie, this is Ezreal, the palace steward. He's pretty much capable of anything."

He laughed. "I don't know about that, but I do try." He gave her a big smile. "It's our honor to have you here, Ms. Caruthers."

Birdie swallowed the mouthful of cocoa she'd just taken. "Oh, honey, call me Birdie, please. That Ms. business is too stuffy. I know this is a palace, and things are done a certain way, but that's one formality I can do without."

"As you wish." He liked her. I could tell by the smile in his eyes. "I've arranged for your quarters to be in the same wing as Princess Jayne and Consort Sinclair. I'll just direct the bellman to take your luggage there, then I'll join you to make sure you have everything you need. Unless there's anything I can get you now?"

I could tell Birdie wanted to ask for something but was hesitant, so I took over, since I had a pretty good idea of what that something was. "I think we could all use a little snack. Some cake, maybe?"

Ezreal smiled. "Tea will be ready in the library in twenty minutes, but I'd be happy to move everything to one of your rooms, if you'd rather have it in a more informal setting."

I looked at Birdie. "What would you like?"

"I think tea in the library sounds wonderful. Then I can see some more of the palace."

"Absolutely." I nodded at Ezreal. "Twenty minutes is great. Just enough time for us to get settled in, then walk over."

"Perfect. See you shortly." He left us to oversee the bellman getting Birdie's luggage, so we headed for the elevator.

As we got into the car, Birdie leaned in. "Is your tea like the English high tea?"

"You mean, will there be food?"

Sinclair laughed knowingly. "Winter elves put the British to shame when it comes to the food served at tea."

Birdie's eyes lit up. "I really am hungry."

I nodded. "Ezreal is out to impress you. There will probably be more food than what we'd normally have, and we normally have enough food that tea could be considered dinner. Probably nothing hot, though, and definitely heavy on the sweets. Remember, this is winter-elf country. There aren't many folks who like to eat more than we do."

Birdie let out a little sigh of relief. "Good. Because werewolves have pretty healthy appetites too."

Sinclair shook his head, still smiling. "You're going to do just fine up here, Birdie."

Somehow, as we strolled down the hall toward our apartments, Ezreal stepped out of the door that led into Birdie's rooms. He smiled at us, hands clasped before him.

"Wow," Birdie said. "You're fast."

He bowed his head. "Just doing my job, Miss Birdie."

She patted his arm. "Well, Mr. Ezreal, you do it very well."

He gestured through the open door behind him. "May I show you your quarters?"

Birdie peeked in. "Is this a whole apartment?"

"Yes, Miss Birdie. There are no single rooms on this floor."

She looked back at me. "Now you're just spoiling me."

"Too much?" I asked.

"Nope." She smoothed the front of her coat and walked in. "Let's have the tour, Mr. Ezreal."

With a little chuckle, Sinclair put his arm around my waist. "She might never leave."

"Not with a grandniece and grandnephew in Nocturne Falls, but I figured if she's comfortable, we'll get to keep her a little longer."

He kissed my temple. "Good plan. How are you feeling?"

"About the skeleton?"

"About having her here. How's your stress level?"

"All things considered, pretty low. But some of that might be because finding a skeleton in the carriage has pretty much taken over the thoughts in my head. Not much room in there for wedding stuff now."

"I'm sure. Still, I'm hoping the missing-persons list will turn up something, and this will all be solved in short order."

"That would be good." But I also had a feeling we were hoping for the impossible. After all, things had a way of getting complicated around me. And with Birdie here, it was inevitable. But I wasn't going to let it bother me. We'd figure it out, like we always did.

And then we'd tackle the wedding stuff.

Ten minutes later, the three of us were headed down to the library for tea. Birdie hadn't stopped talking about how much she loved her rooms since we'd met her in the hall.

I was tickled. I'd wanted this reaction, and she hadn't disappointed me.

We took the long way to the library, which meant forgoing the elevator to walk through the halls and down the main stairs. That gave me a chance to give Birdie a mini tour. I pointed out little interesting facts about the palace, as well as told her who the portraits were of as we passed them.

Here and there, Sinclair added a few tidbits of his own, proof that he'd been paying attention in his classes. I was impressed. He was a fast learner with great retention.

Birdie's excited inhale as we entered the library brought a new smile to Ezreal's face. He stood near the door to greet us, but several footmen were on hand to serve as well. I knew he was following protocol, but we didn't need that much help.

I leaned in. "Why don't you let the footmen go? I think we'd all prefer to serve ourselves."

"As you wish, Princess." He went to handle that.

Birdie was shaking her head slowly. The spread was truly impressive. Three multilevel sandwich carousels, two full cakes, a tray of tartlets and petits fours, a display of cold meats, cheeses, and pickled vegetables with rolls and condiments for sandwich making, a chafing dish of meatballs, another of bite-size quiches, a tray of cookies with at least five varieties, a platter of assorted fudge, and a chocolate fountain with about fifty different things to dip in it. From fruit to bites of pound cake, nothing had been left out.

Ezreal had surpassed my expectations.

As the footmen left and he returned to us, I almost laughed. "You're something else, you know that? You deserve a raise."

He grinned. "I am paid handsomely, Princess."

"Well," Birdie said without taking her eyes off the food, "that's good to hear, because if you orchestrated all this, you're more than worth it."

"Don't wait on me," I said. "Go on, fill a plate, I'm right behind you."

As she and Sin headed for the table, I gave Ezreal's arm a squeeze, then let my smile drop and lowered my voice. "I need to talk to my father later. Do you know where he'll be in half an hour?"

"He'll be in his office until five, but at six he and your mother are taking an evening off. Although I'm sure they wouldn't mind your interruption."

I glanced at the wall clock. It was nearly two. "I'll go by the office directly after we eat."

He shifted slightly, putting his hands behind his back. "Anything I can do to help?"

"As a matter of fact, yes. I need two things. First of all, does the palace keep a missing-persons file?"

He narrowed his eyes. "Not in so many words, but I'm sure I can come up with something for you. Missing from any particular date?"

"Yes. Since my naming ceremony." That was a lot of years to cover, but we had no way of knowing when the skeleton had been placed in the carriage.

His brows rose. "I can do that. But it might not be until tomorrow."

"That's fine. The constable is working on it from her end, too, but I was wondering if there might be any differences in the two files."

"Can I ask what this is in reference to? It might help me to know."

I took a breath. "Please keep this to yourself—"

"Of course."

"We found a skeleton in the Crystal Carriage."

His brows rose, but that was as much reaction as I got from him. Ezreal was a cool customer. "I see. And understand. I'll have that list to you as soon as possible. What's the second thing?"

"I'd like a list of anyone who might have ridden in that carriage since my naming ceremony."

"I can answer that without checking the records. No one. The last people in it were you, your parents, and your aunt and uncle. That's it. The carriage hasn't been used since that day."

"That's what I was afraid of. But in a way, that's good." There was no way any of us was the killer. If there was a killer and this wasn't some weird natural-causes thing.

He nodded. "I'll get to work on that missing-persons info. If there is anything else I can do to help, just ask."

"You know I will. And thanks." He was such a good man and a good friend. I was so happy he'd been promoted to palace steward. "Now I'm going to show that chocolate fountain who's boss."

He smiled. "Enjoy yourself."

I did. So did Sin. But no one enjoyed themselves as much as Birdie did.

45

We ate and talked and ate some more until at last we were down to slices of chocolate mousse cake and coffee.

Birdie added creamer to her cup. "I could get used to this."

Sin patted his stomach. "We don't usually indulge like this."

She grinned. "I figured some of this was for me."

I lifted my cup, which held a mocha latte, and smiled. "I just wanted you to know how much we appreciate your help. Ezreal definitely took it to a new level, though, and I'm glad he did. You dropped everything and came up here on a moment's notice. That's above and beyond. So you deserve some extra special treatment."

She blushed a little. "It's what friends do. You'd do it for me."

"I would."

She sipped her coffee, then set the cup back on the saucer. "We should make a game plan, though. There's a lot of wedding information I need. For example, what do you want me to tackle first?"

I didn't have to think about that at all. "Nothing. Not today. Today I want you to relax and settle in. Then, tomorrow morning, we'll sit down and get serious." I looked at Sin. "Can you get started on giving Birdie a more thorough palace tour? I need to go see my father. I'll join you when I'm done."

He nodded. "I'd love to. What do you think, Birdie? Want to see the palace?"

"Absolutely." Then she laughed. "After all this food, the walking will be good for me."

"About that," he said. "We use Segways."

Her mouth came open. "For real? Those crazy people movers that they give tours of Nocturne Falls on?"

He nodded. "Yep."

"Is the palace that big?"

He snorted. "You have no idea." He lifted his cup. "But you're about to find out."

I fixed a plate of cookies for my dad, because chocolate toffee chip was one of his favorites, then left Sinclair and Birdie to do their tour and headed to his office with the promise that I'd come find them when I was done.

The short walk only took me a few minutes, but I was hustling. On my way, I passed staff working on the palace upkeep. Normally, that was done after hours, when it would also be out of sight, but with the impending wedding and all the visitors that would bring, getting the palace into tiptop shape had become a round-the-clock activity.

Even with the wedding still a few months off.

Not going to lie, I felt a little guilty about so much work being done just because Sin and I were getting married. It was humbling and a great reminder of what an amazing life I led.

The enormity of this event was a little crazy if I let myself really think about it. But I'd arrived at my father's office, and there was a much more important matter to discuss.

I knocked, then went in. Mrs. Greenbaum, the woman Ezreal had hired to take his place as my father's assistant, was at her desk typing away with a headset on. No doubt transcribing something.

She stopped and looked up, removing the headset as I entered. "Good afternoon, Princess."

"Hi, Mrs. Greenbaum." She wasn't Ezreal, but she was wonderful in her own way. Exceptionally organized, quick on the keyboard, and she made the best lingonberry scones I'd ever tasted. "Is my dad in his office?"

"He is." She reached for the intercom with her eyes still on me. "Shall I buzz him for you?"

"No, it's okay. I can just go in. Unless you think he needs the warning."

"He'll be happy to see you." She gave me a little smile and started to slip her headphones back on but left one ear uncovered. "There are scones on his conference table."

"Lingonberry?" She did, on occasion, make other varieties.

"Mm-hmm." She smiled. "With vanilla glaze."

"I picked the right time to visit." I was stuffed from that fabulous tea, but that wasn't going to stop me from having a scone. Then I glanced down at the plate of cookies I'd brought. "I guess he won't want these."

She shook her head. "I bet he will. What father turns down a thoughtful gift like that?"

"That's kind of you. Thank you." I knocked on his door. Behind me, Mrs. Greenbaum started typing again. "Dad? It's me, Jayne."

"Come in, honey," he called out.

I opened the door. "Hey, how are you? Hard at work? I brought you some cookies."

I shut the door behind me, then took a seat across from the slab of glacier he used as a desk. There were three organized stacks of files and papers in front of him. The one directly in front of him was the smallest.

"I'm good. Mostly working hard. This kingdom doesn't run itself, you know."

"I know." Just like royal weddings didn't plan themselves.

"How are you?"

"Better."

He looked at the plate in my hands with anticipation. "Any chocolate toffee chip?"

"That's all I brought."

He patted an empty spot in front of the stacks. "Right there."

As soon as I set the plate down, he took a cookie and bit into it.

My brows went up. I really hadn't expected him

to eat any. Not with Mrs. Greenbaum's scones at his disposal. "You're not stress-eating, are you? What's going on?"

He shook his head and sighed around the mouthful of cookie. "Nothing."

"Which means it's something you don't want to tell me about." I crossed my arms. The little wisps of icy vapor in the air were a sure sign something was bothering him. "What is it? Did you already hear the news?"

His eyes rounded, and I thought I detected the slight hint of panic. "What news? Please tell me you haven't called off the wedding."

"What? No. Why on earth would we do that?"

"Never mind. What's the news?" He lifted the cookie to his mouth again.

"We found a skeleton in the Crystal Carriage."

He stopped midbite. "A real one?"

"Yes. That would have been a pretty sick prank otherwise."

"True." His gaze tapered. "Who is it?"

"No idea, but the constable is searching her missing-persons reports. Ezreal's looking into palace records for the same reason."

"Yikes." He finished the first cookie and took a second one. "I guess that's why you're here."

"Yep." I glanced over my shoulder at his conference table. The plate of scones was within arm's reach, so I helped myself to one. The tart aroma of the lingonberries and the sweet fragrance of the vanilla glaze were already making my mouth water. "I wanted you to hear it from me, not through the grapevine."

"I appreciate that."

"Do you remember anyone being reported missing in the last thirty years?" I bit a pointy end off the scone. It practically melted in my mouth. Amazing.

He thought while he reached for a third cookie. He was definitely stress-eating. Nice to know where I got it from. "Not that comes to mind immediately."

"Like I said, Ezreal is going through palace records to see if he can come up with anything, but if you can't remember anyone, then he probably won't find anything either."

"Do you think the cause of death was accidental?"

The tone of his voice told me that's what he was hoping for. I shrugged. "No idea. But who would accidentally die in the carriage? If it was one of the footmen, we'd have missed him. Really, if it was anyone we knew, we would have missed them."

"True."

"Plus, it was just a skeleton. No clothing. Nothing else."

My father grimaced. "Like it was dumped there?"

"Maybe." I shrugged again, trying to keep things light. "Anyway, the ME is examining the remains, so we should know something soon."

He finished chewing another bite. "Dr. Charming is a good man. A little odd, but good."

I sat up. "Odd how?"

My dad took a fourth cookie. Yep. This was stress-eating at its finest. "You know how highly intelligent people are. A little…cerebral, I guess."

"Huh. Well, he is a doctor."

"Right." My dad shook his head. "Who on earth could that skeleton be?"

"Hopefully, we'll known soon. Hey, while I'm here, I have another question for you. Why did the tours of Hangar Nine stop?"

My father ate half of the cookie in his hand, thinking. "I'm not sure, actually. In fact, I guess I didn't know that they had."

"Well, that's what Tianna told us. She's the one who took us through and handled the approval paperwork for us today. She said it happened before she was hired, and I think she's been there about twelve years."

"I believe that's right." My dad pushed the button on his intercom. "Mrs. Greenbaum?"

She buzzed back. "Yes?"

"See if you can find out why the tours of Hangar Nine were discontinued."

"Yes, Your Majesty."

I loved how things got done around here. "She'll probably have to speak to the school superintendent."

"Probably." My father pointed his cookie at me. "Now *there's* a strange man."

"Oh? How is he strange?" I thought for a moment. "Dr. Bitterbark, right?"

"Yes, and he's well named. Although I don't know if he's bitter exactly, but he's a cold fish. Very walled off, if you know what I mean."

"That's kind of a weird disposition for someone who works with kids. I mean, sure, he's got to oversee the school system and make sure everything is running smoothly and standards are being met, but you'd think he'd be a happy enough sort."

"Right, well, I suppose he's nice to the students, but on a broader social level outside of work, he tends to keep to himself. Not that there's anything wrong with that." My father leaned back. "Some of that might be because he takes care of his mother. Has for years. She's been unwell for nearly as long as he's been working for the North Pole school system. So he really doesn't get out much."

"Unwell how?"

"She's got Grater's lung disease."

I stared at him blankly. "She was a miner?"

"Not that I'm aware of."

"I thought that was exclusive to the elves who worked in the mines."

"It's possible to get it without working there. Some of the bakers get a version of it if they inhale too much flour."

"But like you said, that's a version of it. That's not really Grater's." I lifted one shoulder. "I just think it's odd, that's all."

"You're not wrong. But I'm pretty sure it was Dr. Charming who diagnosed her. You want to tell him his analysis is off?"

"Nope. Not when I need him to concentrate on identifying that skeleton." I ate the last bite of scone and spoke around the crumbs. "So what's really going on that you're eating those cookies like they've been prescribed to you?"

He sighed, then frowned with the realization I wasn't going to let this go. "Your mother. And your aunt. And this wedding."

I barked out a laugh. "Welcome to the club." I lifted my index finger toward the ceiling in triumph. "But my secret weapon arrived today."

"Oh?"

I smiled. "Birdie Caruthers. She's going to wrangle this whole wedding mess into shape. You'll see."

"She does that, and I'll give her the keys to the kingdom."

I stood up, ready to go. "She'd probably settle for the keys to a bakery."

"She can have those too." He cocked one eyebrow. "You really think she can help? Your mother and your aunt are strong forces to reckon with."

I snorted. "Mom and Aunt Martha are like gentle breezes compared to Hurricane Birdie. It's all going to be fine, you'll see. She'll find a way to deal with them that is thoughtful and appropriate and somehow gets me the wedding I want."

"I hope so." He exhaled and another stream of ice vapor curled through the air. "Because at this rate, I'm not going to fit into my suit for the wedding."

I grinned. "I guess I shouldn't have brought you those cookies. And because I love you so much, I'm going to take those scones with me so you won't even be tempted by them."

"Jayne."

I ignored the little warning in his voice and picked up the plate as I headed for the door. "Enjoy your night off with Mom. Have a salad maybe."

I slipped out before he could say another word, then a new thought wiggled into my brain. Barely a thought. A wisp of one not fully formed. I stopped beside Mrs. Greenbaum's desk.

"What can I help you with, Princess?"

I shook my head, trying to capture the tiny seed of an idea that had just come to me. "Hang on..."

But whatever had begun to take shape was gone like the ice vapor in my father's office, leaving me with nothing more than a feeling. I tapped a finger on her desk. "Do me a favor, Mrs. Greenbaum?"

"Anything."

"One, keep making these scones."

She grinned. "Always."

"And two, did you call about the cancellation of the Hangar Nine tours yet?"

"Not yet. Would you like me to do that now?"

"No. Hold off on that until further notice."

6

That half-formed, almost-idea feeling stayed with me on my walk to meet Sin and Birdie, who were already back at our quarters, information I got from asking the various staff members I passed.

But the feeling remained just that—a feeling. I still couldn't name what had made me think now wasn't the right time to dig into the shutdown of the hangar tours. Obviously, a part of my brain thought there was a connection between the ending of the tours and the body in the carriage. Could there be? Sure. But what was it?

I went wild and put the craziest possibility into words. The superintendent had killed whoever that was in the carriage and had then canceled the tours to keep the body undiscovered.

Okay. But that really was crazy. For one thing, if he was the killer, why would he hide the body in the carriage? That wasn't a great hiding spot.

Except that it had been for the last thirty years.

Still, he'd had to realize the body would be discovered now that Sin and I were getting married. Unless he didn't know about the tradition of a royal having to approve the carriage for use. Was that possible? Maybe.

If he thought the carriage was prepared only the week before the event, then he'd think he still had time to move the body. Still an odd place to keep the skeleton of someone you'd murdered. Sure, burying the body was out of the question. The ground was far too hard. A typical NP burial really meant internment into one of the many mausoleums. Cremation was another option. So hiding or destroying the body was the only choice.

Then there was the fact that the superintendent spent all his free time caring for his mother, so because of her, he had a nonexistent social life.

Which brought up the next question. Who on earth could he have killed?

I groaned. All this speculation was just confusing me more. Could it be the superintendent? Yes. But at this point, it could just as well be anybody.

Truth was, we really didn't know anything yet. Once the skeleton was identified, I hoped we'd have a direction to go in. And maybe the half idea would become a full one that made more sense.

I dropped the plate of scones off in my apartment, half expecting to see Sin and Birdie in there. They weren't, so I went over and knocked on Sin's door.

He answered almost instantly, moving aside so I could come in. "Hey. How'd your dad take the news about the skeleton?"

"About as well as could be expected. Better, maybe. Probably because he's pretty distracted with wedding stuff."

Sin made a face. "I hate to think we're interrupting the running of the kingdom."

"Our wedding has become part of running the kingdom. That's just how royal events of this scale go." I sat down on his couch.

"If you say so."

"I do." I gave him a wink, then turned to Sugar, his sweet little white cat, who was curled up on the farthest cushion. I gave her a little scratch. Spider hadn't been around when I'd been in my apartment, meaning he was probably sleeping in the closet. That was one of his favorite hideouts. Sugar was wearing her translation collar that interpreted her vocalizations as words. "How's your day going, Sugar?"

She rolled over and showed me her tummy. "More scratches. More."

I laughed. Sugar didn't have quite the vocabulary that Spider did, but it was improving. "Yes, ma'am." I looked at Sin. "How'd Birdie like the tour?

There's no way you showed her the entire palace. You weren't gone long enough."

"Not even close to half. But after all that food, and the excitement of today, and traveling, she decided she'd rather have a nap, then see the palace at a time when she was awake enough to remember it."

"Yeah, today's already been pretty busy for her." The idea of a nap made me yawn.

Sin laughed. "Maybe you should go lie down too. Do we have plans for tonight?"

"I figured we'd take Birdie into town if she wants to go, but otherwise, no. Don't forget, we start wedding planning bright and early tomorrow morning."

He held his hands up and backed away. "I have class in the morning. Another Royal Daily Life class. So that planning session is all you and Birdie."

I rolled my eyes with a smile on my face. "Men."

He smiled wistfully. "Who knew not being a royal would pay off so handsomely?"

"Let me know if you still feel that way after a couple of hours of that class."

"You know, it's actually been pretty interesting so far. And digging into your family tree has shown me just what kind of crazy to expect from you and at what age to expect it."

I snorted. "I see you've found out about Great-Great-Great-Aunt Lynette?"

"Was she the one who cavorted naked on the tundra?"

I stuck my tongue out at him. "We don't talk about that."

He came over and leaned down, planting a long kiss on my mouth. "First of all, I'm down for naked cavorting if you are. Secondly, I don't care how crazy you get, I'm always going to be nuts about you."

I put my arms around his neck. "We can be nuts together, then."

He leaned in to kiss me again, but a knock at the door interrupted the moment. He kissed me anyway, but it was quick. "I'll get it."

He went to the door while I scratched Sugar some more. It was a footman. "Pardon me, Consort Sinclair. Do you know where Princess Jayne is? I have a note for her."

"She's here. I'll give it to her."

"Thank you, sir." He handed the envelope to Sin, then took his leave.

Sin came back and sat beside me on the couch. "Recognize the handwriting?"

He held the envelope so I could see my name scrawled on the front. "Vaguely familiar, but then again, not really. Open it."

"It's for you."

"So?"

He slid his nail under the seal and took out the note inside. "It's from the constable."

I leaned my head back and stared at the ceiling while still lazily scratching Sugar's fluffy belly. "Read it?"

"Princess, just wanted you to know Dr. Charming has determined that the skeleton is female. No luck with the missing-persons files yet. Larsen."

I picked my head up. "Huh. I wasn't expecting it to be female. Well, I don't know what I was expecting. I need to tell Ezreal. He's searching through palace records to see if he can find a missing person too."

"Well, it eliminates half the population."

I nodded. "I'll run down to his office and tell him."

"You want me to go with you?"

"Absolutely." It would be a great opportunity to tell him about my almost idea. "Although I really don't want to go at all. I'd rather just snooze on the couch."

Sin gave me a look. "You don't have to solve this, you know."

"I know, but I asked Ezreal to help, and I feel like not telling him would make him do double the work. If he knows he only has to look for a missing woman, that would be easier, right?"

"Yeah, it would be. Okay, let's go."

We headed out, and on the way I explained the weird partial thought that had come to me about the hangar tours and not yet digging into the reason for why they were canceled. Then I explained my ideas about the superintendent and why it wouldn't make sense for him to be the killer. If there was a killer. "It's really crazy, right?"

"I don't know if I'd say really crazy. Slightly crazy. But life with you has taught me that crazy in all its forms is possible."

"Well, I'm putting it all on the back burner until we know who this woman is. Then we can reassess."

Sin put his arm around me. "It's cool you brought up the canceled hangar tours to your dad, first of all. But is it weird that he didn't know about it? He's the king. Doesn't all of that kind of stuff eventually make it onto his desk?"

"Yes and no. I mean, the superintendent of schools is like the king of the school system. It's not like he'd have to ask permission to do something like that. But my dad did say the guy is kind of strange. Keeps to himself and not much on social skills, but like I said before, he's also taking care of his very sick mother, so you have to give him some leeway there."

Sin nodded. "Yeah, that has to be hard. What's she got?"

"Grater's lung disease. It's something that I thought only miners got. It's from inhaling the exceptionally cold air in the crystal mines. Winter elves can handle cold, but the mines are so much colder than the regular air, it can sometimes make them sick."

He made a face. "Then why not heat the air in the mines?"

"That was tried. Raising the temperature enough to make a difference caused the crystal to crack and shatter."

He grimaced. "That's too bad."

"It is, but now the miners wear regulators that heat the air before they inhale it. Grater's is pretty rare these days."

"Good to know. How would she have gotten it anyway? And what does the disease do?"

"No idea how. And it diminishes the lung capacity. I imagine she's on oxygen and isn't very mobile. Anything that raises the blood pressure or causes the lungs to work harder just makes breathing worse."

"Wow." He raked a hand through his hair. "That's a terrible way to live. No wonder he's not much for socializing. He's got his hands full caring for her, and I'm sure he wants to spend time with her. Whatever time she has left."

"Agreed." Then I thought about that. "Except for the caring part. As superintendent, he could certainly afford full-time medical care for her. In-home, I mean. But then, maybe he's got that, and he just can't bring himself to leave her for long, because like you said, he wants to spend whatever time she has left with her. Who knows?"

"Right." He stuck his hands in his pockets. "I bet Mamie would know more."

"Oh, you're right. She would." Mamie knew everything about everyone. And if she didn't, she could find it out. She was the North Pole's version of Birdie. And my uncle Kris's secretary. "We need to talk to her. And we should really introduce her and Birdie, since they're so alike."

"Tomorrow after breakfast?" Then he sighed. "But you'll have to go alone. I'll be in class."

"I can do it. I'm sure Birdie will want to say hi to my uncle anyway and see the toy factory. Maybe even see some of the town. You know, that will eat up a big chunk of the day. I'm not sure how much wedding stuff we'll get done."

"A few days of playing tourist with her isn't going to hurt. You can ease into the wedding planning." He smiled. "So long as you do get started on it."

"We will, I promise. Birdie won't let me postpone much longer. And I'm very aware that weddings, royal or otherwise, don't happen overnight. The people involved need time to prepare everything. Even if it is their main project. We're only a few months away now."

We reached Ezreal's door.

Sin turned to me. "It will all get done. No one wants to let you down, and there is plenty of time left for everything to be accomplished. You'll see."

"I know you're right. I just can't help but worry."

He kissed my forehead. "I don't want you to worry. I want you to enjoy our wedding day. It's the only one we get, after all."

I nodded and reminded myself to breathe. "Again, you're right. It'll all get done. And I want us both to enjoy it."

Never in the history of royal weddings had there been one that was anything but a beautiful, perfect day. There was no reason to think ours would be any different.

Except for the dead woman in the carriage.

Because that was very different. And definitely not perfect.

That evening, we took Birdie to Sweetie's, a mom-and-pop diner that did everything right. In the last couple of months, it had become one of Sin's favorite spots. A good substitute for Mummy's, he always said.

We'd called ahead to let them know we were coming, like we always did, mostly as a courtesy to them and so we could get the back-corner booth. It was the most private and the least likely to attract a crowd.

For the most part, Sin and I were left alone, but the closer the wedding got, the more excitement built up. People were charged up about it, and many of them wanted to wish us well. The love and support were amazing, but it was tiring too.

And we didn't want to create issues for the restaurant.

I sat between Birdie and Sinclair, and our server,

the same one we usually had, Jake, brought us glasses of water and menus.

He gave us a little bow. "Welcome to Sweetie's, Princess, Consort, and guest."

"Thank you," Sinclair said for all of us.

Jake smiled. He was an older man and had worked at Sweetie's all of his adult life. It was a good gig. I knew that from one of the palace chefs who had worked here in high school. She always talked about her experience here with glowing remarks. "I'll give you a few minutes to look over the menu, but we do have two specials tonight. Prime rib and honey bourbon-glazed salmon."

"That sounds good," Birdie said.

I nodded. "It's all good. Thanks, Jake."

"Of course, Your Highness." He left us to peruse the menu.

"Seriously, though," Birdie said. "What should I get?"

"You can't go wrong with any of it," Sin said. "The shrimp and lobster pot pie is one of my favorites. The stuffed pork chops are delicious too."

I closed my menu. "So is the butternut squash ravioli, which is what I'm getting, along with a cup of corn chowder."

Birdie groaned. "You're not making this any easier for me."

Sin laughed. "I promise there are no bad choices."

She looked up from her menu. "What are you getting?"

He tapped his finger on the menu. "Something a little different. BBQ bacon burger with cheddar cheese, sweet potato fries and jalapeño coleslaw."

"My mouth is watering." She shook her head. "I hadn't even considered a burger until now. Thanks for nothing."

His grin widened. "The palace kitchen makes a decent burger, but it doesn't compare to what you get here. Just throwing that out there."

Jake came back with a piping-hot dish and set it in the center of the table, then passed out small plates to each of us. "Compliments of the kitchen. Lasagna-stuffed mushrooms. Word of warning, they are very hot."

Birdie leaned in. "I'd say so. The cheese is still bubbling. They smell so good, though."

Jake nodded. "They are. I tried one earlier. Have you decided on what you'd like to eat, or should I give you a few more minutes?"

I answered him. "I don't think Birdie is ready."

She glanced at Jake. "It all looks too good, and I can't decide. What would you suggest for a first-timer?"

"That is a tough one, but..." He pointed to something on her menu. "The Sweetie's sampler is a good choice. One mini shrimp and lobster pot pie, a slice of our famous meat loaf, half of a ham-

and-cheese risotto stuffed pepper and two sides. I'd suggest our bacon horseradish mashed potatoes and minted baby peas, but that's just me."

She closed her menu. "Done." She looked at Sin and me. "You might have to roll me back to the palace, though."

Jake took her menu. "We're happy to box up any leftovers. Just in case you want to save room for the seven-layer tundra cake."

Birdie bit her bottom lip. "I shouldn't ask this, but I'm going to anyway. What's a tundra cake?"

"Our version of black forest. Seven layers of chocolate cake alternating with chocolate mousse, vanilla buttercream, and cherry jam, all covered with dark chocolate ganache."

A little moan came out of her. "I definitely need that." Then she waved a hand at us. "You two go before I add anything else to my order."

Sin and I gave Jake our orders, and as he left to put them in, a little girl approached the table. She couldn't have been more than five or six, her pale blue hair in braids, and she held a piece of paper very close to her jumper.

She did a deep, wobbly curtsy that was about the cutest thing I'd ever seen.

"Hi there," I said.

She rose and looked me in the eyes, as solemn as could be. "Good evening, Princess Jayne."

"Good evening. What's your name?"

"Matilda. I like you a lot."

"That's very kind of you. I like you a lot. Your hair is very pretty."

She grinned, revealing a missing tooth. "Thank you. My mom says you have a cat. I have a cat too. His name is Mr. Boots, because his feet are all white."

"Mr. Boots sounds very handsome. My cat is all black, and his name is Spider. He came with that name. Consort Sinclair has a cat too. Her name is Sugar, and she's all white."

Matilda's smile somehow got bigger. "I love cats."

"Me too. Are you having dinner here with your family tonight?"

"Yes, Your Grace."

Birdie put a hand to her cheek. "The cuteness is too much."

I nodded in agreement. "What can I do for you this evening, Matilda?"

She suddenly went shy. "I drew you a picture."

"You did? Is that the piece of paper you're carrying?"

She nodded.

"Can I see it?"

She nodded again and put the paper on the table, turning it around as she did.

Her crayon drawing was of a wedding cake. It was covered in snowflakes and swirls and all kinds of embellishments and completely extravagant. On top of the cake was a crown. My snowflake tiara, actually. I loved it.

"Wow, that is the best-looking cake I've ever seen. Did you design this yourself?"

"Yes, Your Grace." She was still smiling, but was now also swaying back and forth slightly, hands clasped in front of her.

"Are you going to be a baker when you grow up?"

"Yes, just like my mom and dad. But I want to make cakes. They make cookies."

A woman came up behind her. "Matty, why don't you let the princess enjoy her dinner now, honey?" She smiled at me, bobbing down slightly. "I'm sorry if she's taken up too much of your time."

"Not at all. Matilda and I were just discussing the design she came up with for my wedding cake. It's the best I've seen. I'll be taking it with me to the bakery when we go for cake tasting."

Matilda's eyes went wide. "You will?"

"You better believe it." I looked at Sin. "What do you think?"

He appraised it with a serious eye. "It's everything I've ever wanted in a cake. I say yes."

Matilda started clapping. Her mother looked like she might fall over.

"Thank you so much for this, Matilda," I said. "You have your mom contact the palace steward tomorrow and give him all your details so we can credit you properly, okay?"

Her nod made her braids wiggle. "Yes, Your Grace. Thank you."

Her mother swallowed. "Your Highness, are you serious?"

"Absolutely."

Her expression stayed on utter surprise for a moment more, then changed into shocked disbelief. "That is…so kind of you. Thank you."

"You're welcome. Please do call the palace steward tomorrow so we can have Matilda's information for the records. His name is Ezreal Zur'dar, and I'll tell him to expect your call."

"I will, thank you. Enjoy your dinner."

"You too."

She guided her daughter off. Matilda gave us one last wave over her shoulder.

Birdie shook her head. "Are you really going to use her cake design?"

"You bet I am. It's glorious. Completely over-the-top. All the designs I've seen so far have been beautiful, but a little too restrained. I'm going to send her a basket of goodies for her cat too."

Birdie put her hand over mine. "You're good people, Jayne."

Sin nodded. "Yes, she is."

Now I was on the verge of blushing. "So are you, Birdie."

Jake showed up with our food.

As he distributed it, I leaned closer to him. "There's a table in here with a little girl about six years old, light hair in braids. She's with her family. I'd like to pick up their check."

He put my plate in front of me. "The little girl who drew you a picture?"

"You know about her?"

"Yep. The mom asked if I thought it would be okay if she gave you the drawing. I said yes. I hope that was okay."

"It was more than okay. You'll put their check on the palace account?"

"I will."

"Thank you."

"You're welcome." He stood back. "I hope you enjoy your dinners. I'll be back to check on you in a little bit. In the meantime, is there anything else I can bring you?"

"Not unless you have another kid out there who's got ideas for my wedding dress."

"Sorry, Your Highness. Can't help you there."

I shrugged. "Can't blame a girl for trying."

The next morning at breakfast, we all agreed we were still full. Didn't stop any of us from eating, though. But I noticed we all made lighter selections.

And by lighter, I meant I had only two blueberry pancakes and not three. Also, two sausage links and a fruit cup, but then, breakfast was the most important meal of the day.

As the meal wound down, Sin drained his coffee cup, picked up his last slice of toasted and buttered pumpkin bread, then rose from the table. "I hope you ladies have a wonderful day. I'm off to my class. Will I see you for lunch?"

I shook my head. "I don't think so. I want to take Birdie to the cafeteria at the factory. Hopefully, with Mamie and my uncle."

"Sounds like fun. Wish I could join you, but my higher education awaits." He winked as he came around and kissed me. "I'll see you this afternoon, then, and you can catch me up on the wedding progress you've made."

Birdie patted the notebook next to her plate. "And there will be progress."

He laughed. "I'll believe it when I see it."

"Oooh," Birdie said with a snicker and a wiggle of her brows. "A challenge."

I shooed him away. "Out with you. She's going to work me like a dog, now."

He snorted. "She was already going to work you like a dog."

Birdie tipped her head almost apologetically. "We do have a lot to do."

Bread in hand, Sin headed for the door. "I'm out of here."

I sighed as I looked at Birdie. "Should I even ask what you're going to make me work on today?"

"We need to set up a few basic things. Your likes and dislikes, what vendors you're using, a copy of the guest list, that kind of stuff. Then I can get to work."

"Ezreal can get you a copy of the guest list. Very little of that is up to Sin and me. A lot of it is political. That's just how these kinds of royal events work."

"I understand that. But what about the rest of it?"

"Whatever you need."

"Great." She put her hand flat on the notebook. "Because I'd like to get as much of that done now. Is that possible?"

"Sure. I do need to go over to the factory, though. Not only do I need to talk to Mamie and want to introduce you to her, but I think you'll really enjoy seeing the place."

"I am definitely looking forward to it." She smiled. "Just being here is like something out of a dream, but actually getting to see where the toys are made? And see the workers making them? I cannot wait."

"Then let's get another cup of coffee and get cracking on the wedding game plan." I couldn't believe I was volunteering myself so freely, but the more info Birdie had, the more she could organize.

An hour and a half later, my brain felt like it had been wrung out. Birdie had asked me more questions than I could count. She'd filled I didn't know how many pages in her notebook. At this point, she probably knew more about my wedding preferences than I did.

Our breakfast plates had been cleared a while ago, which was good because I needed the space in front of me to rest my head. I even closed my eyes. Possibly groaned a little. "Birdie, I know you need all this information, but I can't take anymore."

"That's okay, you did great. I've got lots to work with. We can be done for now."

"Thank you. My brain hurts," I mumbled into the tablecloth.

"Hush now. You're fine. You want a nice wedding? This is what it takes. Information, planning, organization, and action." I heard her close the notebook. "This is enough to get me started."

I finally looked up at her. "Started? You mean there will be more?"

"Of course. There will be selections to make as things come up. You'll see."

I sighed. Then I smiled as I rested my head in my hands. "Thank you for doing all this. I really do appreciate it."

She smiled back. "I know you do. And it's going to be fun. I promise." Then her brows lifted. "Can we go to the toy factory now?"

I sat up, renewed by the thought of a nonwedding activity. And a chance to dig deeper into the mysterious skeleton incident. "Let's roll."

I used one of the housephones to tell the valets we'd need a crawler ready, then Birdie and I went back to our rooms to get our jackets. I needed to give Spider some extra loves too. With Birdie being here and all the wedding stuff and the remains-in-the-carriage stuff, I'd been busy. I didn't want him to feel like he wasn't getting enough attention.

"Spider?" I called out as I entered my apartment. "Mama's back from breakfast. Come here, baby."

He came trotting in from the other room and sat down in front of me, then meticulously licked one paw like it was super important. "Spider bored."

"I know, baby. I haven't been here much to play with you. And I'm heading out again now. You want to hang out with Sugar today?"

He stopped licking his foot. "Spider likes Sugar."

"I know you do, sweet boy. Come on, let's go across the hall."

He stood up, clearly excited. "Mama, Spider likes boo mouse."

Boo mouse was what Spider called the little catnip-stuffed ghost toy I'd gotten him for Halloween. "Okay, we'll take boo mouse with us. Except I don't know where it is."

"Spider get." He scampered off and came back a minute later with the toy in his mouth.

"Great. Let's go see what Sugar is up to." I took the ghost from him, then scooped him up in my arms. He butted his head against my chin. I kissed his furry head.

A knock sounded at my door. "Jayne? It's me."

Birdie. "Come in, it's open."

She walked through and smiled at the sight of Spider. "Hello there, you handsome little man."

"Spider loves Birdie."

That got a shocked look from both of us. Birdie knew Spider could talk, but for him to say he loved her? I gave Birdie a look. "I see you've made a big impression on him."

I turned him a little so I could see his face. "That's so sweet, baby. You must remember Birdie from when she catsat you."

"Spider remember. Birdie nice."

She scratched his head. "You're nice too, Spider."

That earned her a little trill of affection.

"I'm taking him to Sinclair's to spend the day over there," I told Birdie. "Sin's cat, Sugar, and Spider are best buds."

"Sugar nice," Spider said. Then his little nose twitched. "Sugar pretty."

"Yes, she is. And I bet she thinks you're very handsome too. Just like Mama does."

He pushed his head against my face again.

I laughed, petting him some more. "Funny boy."

Birdie shook her head. "That is the most adorable thing."

"Which reminds me. Spider and Sugar are going to ride in the carriage with me to the ceremony, then back with Sin and me. They have special collars they're going to wear too."

Her brows went skyward. "You're sure about this?"

"Yes." I put a little firmness in the word. "They're very important to us, and we want them included."

"You know that phrase herding cats?"

"Spider and Sugar will be perfectly behaved." I looked at Spider. "Won't you? You're going to do a good job at the wedding, aren't you?"

"Spider gets a bow tie?"

"Yes, Spider gets a bow tie, and Sugar gets a ruffle." I glanced at Birdie. "They aren't going to do anything but ride in the carriage and let people see them. And they'll be in the pictures."

"Well, it'll be cuter than a June bug in a jumpsuit if they can behave themselves."

"They will." I gestured with my elbow. "Birdie, can you get my leather jacket out of the closet there?" I still hadn't grabbed it, and our badges to get into the factory were in the pocket.

"Sure thing."

"Great, thanks. We'll get Spider settled in, and then we're off."

Which was exactly what we did before heading to the south exit.

"Before I forget..." I pulled the two badges out of my jacket pocket as we walked down the hall. Ezreal had messengered hers to me via footman first thing this morning. I'd returned the footman to him with a note about Matilda's mother calling. I held out the laminated rectangle. "You'll need this to get in."

"A badge? Cool. Hey, it has my picture on it."

"Yeah, I told Ezreal to swipe the one from your Facebook profile. I hope that was okay."

"Sure." She grinned. "Except I gave myself a little Photoshop help on this picture. If they look too closely, they might think it's my younger sister."

I laughed. "I promise they'll recognize you."

We exited the palace, jumped into the waiting crawler, and took off. The sky was blue, the sun was shining, and the snow sparkled like diamonds. It was a glorious day in the NP. I pointed out a few interesting places as I drove, taking my time so Birdie could see everything, but we still arrived at the factory within fifteen minutes.

The guard at the factory gate greeted me with a kind smile. "Morning, Your Highness."

We flashed our badges as I greeted him. "Good morning."

He lifted the gate. "Have a good day."

"You too."

I parked in the designated royal reserved space, mostly to impress Birdie, and we got out. My uncle's cherry-red crawler was two spots over. "Don't put your badge away yet. You'll need it at this entrance too."

But we didn't make it beyond the sidewalk when Birdie stopped.

Hands on hips, she tilted her head back to get a better look at the building. "It's shaped like a Christmas tree."

"That, it is."

"So cool." She grinned as we started walking again. "I have a feeling this is going to be good."

"I certainly hope it lives up to your expectations."

"It will. It already has."

"Don't expect too much at first. This entrance isn't as fancy as the main one, but that's because it's more utilitarian. This one gets us onto the express elevator that goes straight to the top and my uncle's office." We entered the small steel and glass foyer. Beyond that was a locked metal door leading to the rest of the building. A guard sat inside a booth behind an open sliding glass window.

He stood as soon as I entered. "Good morning, Your Highness. And visitor."

"Good morning. We're here to see my uncle." I showed my badge to the guard, then Birdie held hers up too.

"Of course." The guard inspected them, then nodded. "Thank you." He hit a button on the desk, a chime sounded, and the metal door slid back. The hall was as simple and austere as the foyer, but that décor would change as we got deeper into the building.

"You're right," Birdie said. "This isn't what I expected after the building's exterior."

"Just wait," I said as we reached the elevators. I pushed the Up button.

The doors opened to reveal the plush interior that hinted at what was to come.

Birdie touched the gold trim and tufted burgundy velvet paneled walls as we walked in. "This is fancy. And more in keeping with what I expected."

With the fabric walls and the dark wood panels on the lower half, the space had a warm, cozy vibe. I tapped the S button, then tilted my head toward the back wall of glass. "You might want to watch."

"In the mirror?"

"It's not a mirror."

Birdie looked closer, and as the elevator rose and the first level of the factory floor came into view, a happy little gasp slipped from her lips.

"Wow."

Elves by the thousands labored at their workstations, all of them building the toys that my uncle would place under Christmas trees around the world on the night of December twenty-fourth. The workers moved with such deft speed that shimmering remnants of magic spiraled into the air.

Eyes wide, Birdie braced herself on the railing in front of the glass and leaned in. "This is remarkable. I've never seen anything like it."

"You never will anywhere else either. Elf magic is what makes such production possible."

As we went higher, more levels came into view. Robots were being assembled on one. Stuffed animals were sewn on another. Puzzles and games were boxed on a third.

Farther and farther up we went. Birdie stayed glued to the windows, then her eyes narrowed. "Do I hear singing?"

"You do. It's kind of a thing we do while we work."

She looked at me. "So that's not just a made-up thing in fairy tales?"

"Not at all. Singing keeps spirits light, makes the time go by, and keeps all the workers connected to each other. And it's fun."

She looked skeptical. "Do you do it?"

I knew where this was headed. "Sometimes."

"So you can sing?"

That was the question I'd been expecting. "All elves can sing. Some better than others, but all generally well. You'll see. There will be singing at the wedding." Which reminded me that Sin and I hadn't picked our official song yet.

Birdie's mouth bent in obvious amusement. I raised my brows at her expression. "Excuse me, don't all you werewolves howl at the moon?"

She barked out a laugh. "I suppose we do."

I jerked my thumb toward the window. "There's more to see."

She turned back. And blinked as she peered closer. "Are those slides?"

I nodded. "Quickest way to get down from the upper floors."

"I have got to try that. Can I?"

"Absolutely." I grinned. I was so happy she was enjoying herself.

The elevator stopped, and we got off at my uncle's office. I held my hand out. "Welcome to Santa Claus's office."

Mamie looked up from her desk as we walked in. "Hello, Princess Jayne."

"Hi there, Mamie. How are you?"

"Just fine." She put down the paper she'd been holding and got to her feet. Today's outfit was a celadon-green twinset with a navy pencil skirt. As always, a slim strand of North Pole crystal beads, a gift from Uncle Kris on her fiftieth anniversary of employment, glittered at her throat. "What brings you by today?"

"I have a guest in town, and I wanted to introduce you." I put my hand on Birdie's arm. "This is Birdie Caruthers from Nocturne Falls. She's the same kind of amazingly resourceful woman that you are and has helped me out many times in Nocturne Falls, so I thought you two ought to know each other. Birdie, this is Mamie Wynters."

Mamie smiled and came out from behind the desk, hand extended. "It's a pleasure to meet you, Birdie."

Birdie took her hand. "And you, Mamie. What an amazing job it must be to work here. I bet you have stories to tell."

Mamie laughed. "Oh, do I. What do you do in Nocturne Falls?"

"I handle the front desk at the sheriff's department. My nephew is the sheriff."

"How about that?" Mamie exclaimed. "You must be so proud. And talk about stories to tell. We should do lunch sometime while you're here."

"That would be great."

I was reluctant to interrupt the blossoming new friendship, but the timing was too good. "I was actually hoping we could have lunch today. The four of us. At the cafeteria."

Mamie nodded. "We should do that. Your uncle would love to spend some time with you. Unfortunately, he's reviewing some new go-kart designs at the test track right now and will probably be there all day."

"Rats. I really was hoping we could all go."

Mamie clasped her hands in front of her. "We could still go. The three of us."

"That would be great. Since we've got some time before lunch, why don't I give Birdie a tour of the factory? Then we'll be back, and we can all head to the cafeteria."

"Perfect. That will let me get this paperwork done." Then she hesitated. "There's something else, though, isn't there? Another reason you came by?"

"Well…" I explained about the female skeleton in the carriage and the search for a matching missing person and the chance the school superintendent was somehow involved, then took a breath. "With everything you know about this town and the people who live here, what do you think?"

Mamie's left brow arched slightly higher than her right.

Birdie grinned. "You know something, don't you?" She looked at me. "She knows something."

Mamie relaxed her brow and shrugged nonchalantly. "I know Finnoula."

I squinted at her. "Who's Finnoula?"

"Mrs. Bitterbark. George's mother." Mamie leaned in. "And between us, there's something off about her illness. Something not quite right."

"Such as?" I asked.

Mamie paused. "All I can say is I don't think she's as sick as she makes out to be."

The best part of the factory tour was the start of it—from the top floor of my uncle's office, we took the slide all the way down to the bottom.

Birdie went first. I heard a little scream that started out sounding panicked, then turned into one of exhilaration. When I met her at the bottom, she was giggling like I had never before heard her. She put her hand on her stomach. "My lands, that was fun. But I think once was enough."

I snorted as I smoothed a hand over my hair to make sure I wasn't too disheveled. "Well, it's all up from here anyway."

The tour of the factory took a little over two hours, in part because there was so much to see, but also because Birdie wanted to talk to so many of the workers. She gave a lot of praise for the jobs they were doing, and she asked a lot of questions. I loved that about her, though. I was a question-asker myself.

Asking questions was the only way to learn, and the fact that she was so interested in everything made me appreciate her that much more. She wasn't faking her curiosity about my town. It was all genuine. Hard not to love a person like that.

Despite everything we saw and everyone we met, I suspected part of Birdie's mind was stuck on the same thing mine was. The little nugget of info Mamie had dropped on us about Finnoula Bitterbark.

What did it mean in the scheme of things that she might not be as sick as she let on? Why pretend otherwise? There were myriad reasons, of course, but if Mamie was right, Finnoula was certainly committed to her ruse. My father had said she'd been sick for years. But I guess faking an illness like Grater's wasn't something you could just stop doing.

Grater's wasn't curable.

So she either genuinely had it, maybe not in such an advanced stage as was believed, or she was an incredible actress and was now stuck pretending to be sick. There was always an out, of course. Coming clean and fessing up. But that would mean admitting her lie.

And what would the repercussions of that be for her son, the superintendent?

I couldn't wait for lunch and the answers I hoped it would bring.

Birdie hooked her arm through mine as we

approached the elevator. "Thank you for bringing me here and showing me all of this. Charlie would love this. I wish I could tell him about it."

"You could. The North Pole isn't exactly a secret. Maybe leave out the part about how to get here." Charlie was her nephew and one of the cutest little werewolves you'd ever seen. "Does he still believe in Santa?"

"Oh yes," Birdie assured me. "And he will for the rest of his life if I have anything to say about it. Hannah Rose too. Although she's still kind of little to understand the Santa thing."

Hannah Rose was Charlie's baby sister, the newest addition to the Merrow family. "How old is she now?"

"Almost two."

We got on the elevator and went back up to my uncle's office. "Maybe someday you could bring them up to visit. You and Jack. If Ivy and the sheriff wouldn't mind letting the kids go on a trip without them."

"Maybe." Birdie nodded as we got out of the car. "Or maybe before that, your uncle could do a special appearance in Nocturne Falls."

"We can certainly talk to him about it. Having Santa visit the toy shop would be perfectly logical too."

Santa's Workshop was the toy store chain owned by my family. The one in Nocturne Falls was our flagship location. I'd worked there as the manager until moving back here. The stores allowed my uncle to do all kinds of product testing and field research.

Mamie was on the phone when we went into the office, but she hung up a few moments later and smiled brightly at us. "How did you enjoy your tour, Birdie?"

"It was magical. I love this place."

"I'm so glad you enjoyed it. Ready to eat?"

Birdie laughed. "Mamie, I'm a werewolf. We're always ready to eat."

"Then let's go."

"We're taking the elevator, right?" Birdie asked. "I don't think the slide before lunch is such a great idea."

I squelched my urge to chuckle. "Yep, elevator it is."

Mamie closed up the office, and we headed down to the cafeteria. "I'm not a slide person either," she told Birdie. "I mean, look at me. Do I look like a woman who travels by slide?"

Birdie and I both shook our heads. Mamie, in her pencil skirt and twinset, clearly wasn't dressed for that kind of tomfoolery. Or any kind of tomfoolery, really. That's probably why she was so good at keeping things under control up here.

The cafeteria was hopping for lunch, but there was a table reserved for my uncle, so seating wouldn't be a problem. We took our trays and got in line. The smells were all so yummy, but once again, we were faced with far too many selections.

"How am I going to choose?" Birdie asked, moving to the side to see past people. "This is Sweetie's all over again. And I'm sure it's all good."

"It is," Mamie said. "But one of today's specials is a patty melt on rye with fries, and it's an absolute favorite of mine, so I'm getting that. Especially with a slice of cherry pie a la mode to finish it off."

Birdie's mouth rounded. "And here I thought you were going to get a salad. Nice to be proved wrong."

Mamie smiled. "I may dress like a lady, but I eat with gusto. And the patty melt is not to be missed."

"That does sound good. A patty melt and cherry pie are both classics. Hard to go wrong there."

"Except," I added with my finger raised for emphasis, "that they also have tater tot casserole as a special today, and banana pudding is one of the desserts. So I don't even need to see what else is on the menu."

"Oh my." Birdie looked around. "Where are you seeing these specials?"

I pointed out the board where they were listed, along with the day's soups, which were split pea with ham and crab chowder, and the daily desserts of cherry pie, banana pudding, and carrot cake.

Birdie took a moment to read the board, then

shook her head. "Way too much to pick from, but I'm going to compromise and get a patty melt and banana pudding."

"Perfect," I said.

We got our food and sat in the reserved booth. I never minded anyone coming up to me because of who I was, like Matilda at Sweetie's, but that never happened in this cafeteria. People here were pretty used to seeing me. And this was their lunch hour. Most of them wanted to catch up with their friends, enjoy their break, and relax for a few. Not get an autograph from the princess.

We dug into our meals, letting a few minutes of silence go by while we enjoyed the food. But then I was ready to dig into something else entirely.

"All right, Mamie. Tell us what you know about Finnoula."

"Well…" She gestured dramatically with one of her French fries. It wore a cap of ketchup like a little hat. "It seems George had his heart broken once upon a time in the blossom of his youth. He was devastated. He'd planned to marry the girl, and she ditched him cold. Never even returned the ring, from what I've heard. He fell into such a funk that Finnoula decided to give him something else to focus on."

Mamie delicately bit the ketchup hat off the fry.

Birdie's mouth gaped. "Are you saying she made up the illness so he'd take care of her?"

Mamie swallowed. "She didn't make it up. She's definitely sick. But something—call it instinct, call it a woman's intuition, whatever you like—but something tells me she's dramatizing this disease. Milking it for all it's worth."

"But Dr. Charming diagnosed her," I said. "He would know if she was putting on a show."

"Sure, to some extent. He can test her lungs and see if the disease is present, but can you tell a fake cough from a real one? If someone's truly weak or just acting weak? A test for lung capacity in a Grater's patient can be affected by the effort the patient puts in. There's a lot to a disease like that which can be amplified by the person who has it."

I thought about that. "And how many years has she had Grater's?"

"I'd say at least thirty. Maybe longer." Mamie squinted in deep thought. "It wasn't so bad for the first decade or so. She still made it to our canasta games then. But as time went on, the disease progressed." She shrugged. "Or her portrayal of it did."

Birdie looked at me. "Didn't you say Grater's is a disease that the miners get? That it involves long exposure to extreme cold?"

I nodded. "Right. That's why I don't know how Finnoula could have gotten it."

"It happens," Mamie said. "Once in a while, if

an elf is a little frail. She could have had some other illness as a child that made her more susceptible to it."

"Oh? I don't think I knew that."

"Sure," Mamie said. "Shiver pox, for example."

"But we've all had shiver pox."

"Hold up," Birdie said. "What's shiver pox?"

"Three days of spots, itching, and nonstop shivering," I answered. "The winter elf version of chicken pox. We all get it around age five or six. Once you have it, you're immune to ever having it again. And a lot of elves believe it strengthens your constitution against things like Grater's."

"It does," Mamie said. "Except in a few rare individuals. In those cases, it makes them more likely to get certain illnesses. That's why miners have to go through so many tests before they're cleared for the mines."

I shook my head. "You learn something new every day." But the idea that Finnoula would go to such lengths for her son was pretty interesting stuff. It also made me wonder just how bad his breakup had been.

And what had happened to the woman who'd dumped him?

I tilted toward Mamie. "Can you tell me anything more about George's breakup? Was he upset enough to want revenge?"

"As in would he have killed his former fiancée

because she ditched him? I don't think so. As far as details..." She squinted in thought, then shook her head. "It was so long ago. I don't think I can recall much more about his state of mind except that he was laid low by the whole thing."

I sighed. "I'd really like to know more."

"Such as?" Birdie asked.

"Such as why George's fiancée left him. Who was she? Does she still live in the North Pole? When did she break up with him? Right after he asked her to marry him or after a long engagement? Did Finnoula approve of the relationship? If not, why not? Has George been involved with any other women since then, or has caring for his mother really consumed all of his free time? And does any of this have anything to do with the hangar tours being shut down?"

Birdie nodded. "All good questions. All questions I'd like the answers to as well. Seems to me a visit to Finnoula is in order."

Mamie clucked her tongue. "You two are—"

"Oh, come on," I said. "You're not curious?"

Her brow went up again. "I was going to say you two are not going over there without me."

I grinned. "You want to go with us?"

"Not only do I want to, but you need me. Finnoula will talk to me. She has to. She owes me."

"That might be true," Birdie said. "But we can't just walk into her house and start asking questions.

Not without some kind of reason. And what does she owe you for?"

"Actually, as a member of the royal family, I sort of could just walk in and start asking questions. But that's not a great way to get answers. However…" I tapped my fingers on the table and smiled. "I think I have a reason."

As much as I wanted to ask what Mamie meant by Finnoula owing her, I didn't. Which wasn't to say I wouldn't reopen that subject at a later date, but right now, we had a bigger pile of snow to shovel.

The drive to the Bitterbarks didn't take long. They lived in the builders' section of town. George's father had been an architect. When Finnoula got sick, George had moved back into his childhood home to take care of his mother. He hadn't lived on his own since. That's what Mamie told us on the drive over, after I filled her and Birdie in on my plan.

When we arrived, we let Mamie go up the steps ahead of us, figuring that since she knew Finnoula, it made sense for her to do the introductions. Although, in all honesty, we weren't sure Finnoula would answer the door. We hoped she would, obviously, but she was supposed to be sick. What did that mean for her mobility? As far as we knew, her illness just made her housebound. Not bedridden.

But we also really hoped George *didn't* answer.

As Mamie rang the bell, I crossed my fingers that this little plan worked. Birdie and I stood a step behind her so that Finnoula would see Mamie's face first. This was one time when being the princess might not help.

The faint melody of the doorbell chimes could be heard on our side, but then nothing. No footsteps. No sounds of movement.

Birdie shrugged. "Maybe she's sleeping. Or at a doctor's appointment."

Mamie rang the bell again. "She's home. She's always home. From what I've heard, she hasn't stepped out of this house in nearly fifteen years. Maybe longer."

Birdie let out a little whistle.

Another four minutes proved Mamie right when the door opened, and a middle-aged woman in a housekeeper's uniform answered. Beneath her white cap, her dark blue hair showed streaks of silver. "Can I help you?"

"I'm Mamie Wynters, an old friend of Finnoula's." Then she stepped to the side. "And this is—"

The housekeeper curtsied and finished her sentence for her. "Princess Jayne."

"And," Mamie continued, "her guest, Birdie Caruthers."

I took it from there. "We're here to see the superintendent. I have a request for him. Official royal business."

"I'm sorry." Lines of concern bracketed the housekeeper's mouth and eyes. Official royal business wasn't something to stand in the way of. "But he's not home. He should be at his office shortly."

Mamie held a notebook to her chest. There was nothing in it, but it made her look official. Like she'd been authorized to accompany me on this errand. Which she had been. By me. "They told us there that he was home for lunch."

"He was," the housekeeper said. "He comes home every day to check on his mother. But he's just gone back."

Exactly as Mamie had said, and thanks to her, we'd timed this perfectly. I smiled my best royal smile. "The request I wish to speak to him about is slightly personal, which is why I thought it would be nice to talk to him at home."

"Of course." The housekeeper nodded sympathetically. "I can leave a message for him if you'd like."

I kept my smile in place. "When do you think he will be home?"

"Usually right at five."

That gave us plenty of time to accomplish what we'd come for.

"Since we're here," Mamie said, "I'd love to say hello to Finnoula. We've known each other for years."

The housekeeper hesitated, glancing over her shoulder like she needed approval.

"That would be very nice," I said. Then I spoke to the housekeeper. "I understand she's not well. Does she get many visitors?"

"Not many, no. Well, none, really," the housekeeper conceded. "Let me see if she's up for company."

But before the housekeeper could go check, Finnoula appeared behind her. She was thin but not gaunt, although her loose sweater over wide-legged pants hid much of her shape. She was a little pale, but when was the last time she'd been outside? She didn't look remotely like a woman at death's door.

Sick, yes. Dying, no. Although the oxygen tank on wheels hooked to the air line tucked over her ears and under her nose was about as convincing as it got.

She stopped at the entrance to the foyer. "I heard voices." She squinted at us. "Mamie? Mamie Wynters?"

"Hello, Finnoula." Mamie stepped through the door. "How've you been?"

Finnoula smiled and took a deep, ragged breath. "As well as I can be. My word, it's been an age. How are you?"

"Very well, thank you. It's lovely to see you."

"You too. You still work for the big man?"

"I do. As a matter of fact, I've brought his niece with me." Mamie moved slightly, gesturing to me as she did.

Finnoula's gaze followed Mamie's pointing. Her eyes widened a little, and she reached out to take hold of the wall, using it to aid her in a shallow bow. "Princess Jayne. What an unexpected honor."

I smiled. "Hello, Mrs. Bitterbark. We came to talk to George, but since he's not here, Mamie was wondering if you'd like some company, seeing as how you two are old friends."

"That would be nice." Finnoula looked at the housekeeper. "Elma, fix a tea tray and bring it into the sitting room, will you?"

"Certainly, Mrs. Bitterbark."

Finnoula waved us on in. "Let's go into the sitting room. I don't have the energy to stand for very long these days."

Mamie came alongside and looped her arm through Finnoula's. The kind, sweet gesture seemed like one of both friendship and support, and Finnoula leaned into her.

I had a good feeling we were going to find out what we'd come for.

We all got seated, and I introduced Birdie, then we made some small talk about her being here to help with the wedding. Right about then, Elma came in with a tea cart that held far more than tea.

Of course, we'd just had lunch, but it would be rude not to take something. We filled our small plates from the selection of little caramel cakes, white-iced brown cookies, slices of cranberry walnut bread, pumpkin muffins, and an assortment of chocolates, salted nuts, and dried fruits.

The abundance wasn't unusual. Most homes in the North Pole were equipped to handle visitors on short notice. Our hospitality was something we prided ourselves on.

But I already knew from my father that George's social life was nonexistent. And Elma had made it clear Finnoula wasn't getting a lot of visitors. Or any. So the spread told me something else. Finnoula either still had an appetite, or George was keeping the house well stocked in an effort to get her to eat.

I wasn't sure I'd be able to tell which, but Finnoula filled her plate along with the rest of us. Whether or not she'd eat what she'd taken remained to be seen.

I took a bite of one of the iced cookies. "These are really good. What are these?"

Finnoula smiled. "Molasses nutmeg sugar cookies with vanilla icing. My own recipe. Elma makes them now. George's father and I always loved them, although George never cared for them." Her smile turned wistful with a memory she didn't share.

The small talk continued while we picked at the food and sipped our tea. Finnoula ate as much as the rest of us, joining in the conversation without any real sign of fatigue. She coughed once or twice while laughing at something, but other than that, she didn't seem terribly unhealthy. Maybe a little tired.

Mamie was telling us a story about a mutual friend of theirs, but when that was over, she took the conversation in a different direction.

She helped herself to a chocolate truffle rolled in coconut flakes. "How's George doing? He works an awful lot, doesn't he?"

"He's doing well," Finnoula answered. "And yes, he does work a lot. He enjoys his job, though."

"That's good." Mamie nodded. "Is he seeing anyone?"

Finnoula hesitated ever so slightly. "Not that I know of. But I'm sure he'd tell me if he was."

"Whatever happened to that woman he was engaged to? Rochelle? Roxanne? What was her name?"

Finnoula's hesitation lasted longer this time. "Rachel."

"That's right." Mamie nodded like it was all coming back to her. I hoped it was. "What ever happened to Rachel? She's still in town, isn't she? Or did she move?"

"I don't know," Finnoula said. "I haven't kept up with her since she abandoned my son. Haven't talked to her at all. If I'm being honest, I don't want to talk to her. After what she did to George, she's dead to me." She stared at her hands in her lap and took another of those long, ragged breaths that made me want to clear my throat.

But her phrasing had Mamie, Birdie, and me giving each other hard looks.

None of us spoke, however, and a long moment of silence passed. It made me think Mamie was using the trick my father had taught me about letting the other person speak first. It always worked for him, and it had always worked for me.

Finnoula opened her mouth, proving that it was about to work this time too. "She broke George's heart, you know. Shattered it."

We all nodded but kept quiet.

Finnoula wasn't done. "He loved her so dearly. You should have seen the ring he bought her. A beautiful orangey-yellow sapphire cut square with tiny diamonds around it and down the band. And that was well before he was making the kind of salary he is now. He said it reminded him of the sun, and since Rachel was his sun, it was perfect."

"It sounds lovely," Mamie said softly. "Why did they break up?"

Finnoula's gaze was as distant as the memories she was lost in. "I don't know. And I didn't want to pry. I just know that she stopped taking his calls. Stopped talking to him. Just removed herself from his life. Didn't even have the decency to return that ring. He was devastated."

She shook her head like she was trying to rid herself of those memories. "He won't talk about it, and I don't want to dredge up that old pain, so I don't bring it up."

"That's understandable," Birdie said. "You don't need the stress of it either. Not with your health."

Finnoula's smile was thin. "A lot of people think I made up my illness to occupy my son's time. So he couldn't dwell too much on what that awful woman did to him."

We weren't expecting her to mention that. I might have been holding my breath.

Finnoula lifted her chin. "Well, I didn't make it up."

"Of course you didn't," Mamie said.

Finnoula's smile flattened. "I'd found out I had Grater's right after he met Rachel. But I kept it a secret. He was so happy, and I didn't want anything to get in the way of that. But when she left him such a broken man, I was concerned he'd go off the deep end without some new purpose in his life. So I gave him that purpose. I told him about my illness. It was the hardest thing I've ever done. I think the stress of it all actually made the disease worse."

She sighed. "I didn't want to be a burden on him, but I didn't want to lose him to the darkness he was falling into. And trust me, he was falling. Fast."

I glanced around. I was pretty sure Birdie and Mamie were on the same page with me in thinking that Finnoula had been between a glacier and a hard place. It made me reconsider everything I'd thought about her up to this point. I sympathized with her. To see her son so hurt and feel like the only way to save him was to give him another heartbreak to focus on... What kind of pain had that caused her?

Mamie took her hand. "We all would have done the same thing."

Finnoula suddenly looked a lot frailer than she had earlier. She glanced at me. "Please, Your Highness, don't say anything to George. In fact, please don't say anything about any of this. His ex, my illness, none of it. He's a sensitive soul, and he does so much for me. He's my whole world. I just don't want him upset."

"Of course. I wouldn't dream of it."

"Thank you." She seemed to relax. Then her brow furrowed. "What was it you came to speak to him about, anyway, if you don't mind me asking?"

I watched her face carefully. "I came to talk to

him about starting up the Hangar Nine tours again. Not just for schoolchildren, but for anyone who'd like to see it. With our pending wedding, I thought it would be the perfect time for people to be able to view the Crystal Carriage up close."

She smiled broadly, and an odd light shone in her eyes. Was it hurt? Longing? I couldn't tell. "I think that's a marvelous idea. I'd like to see it myself, actually. I'd like to see all the vehicles kept there. I hear there's quite a collection of retired sleds. You know my late husband was an architect. He worked on some of the designs for those hangars after the storm of 1896 damaged the original ones."

I shook my head. "I had no idea. That must have been something to watch them being built."

She shrugged. "I've never seen the hangars or been in one. I was too busy raising our children."

"Oh?" This was new information. "George has siblings, then? What do they do?"

"Yes, a brother and a sister. One's a chef. The other works part time in a florist's shop. Both live in the...mortal...world." She put a hand to her chest and took a wheezy, shuddering breath, then started coughing.

The housekeeper came running in. "Mrs. Bitterbark, are you all right?"

I stood. I'd wanted to ask if she knew why George had stopped the tours, but that moment was gone. "We should go. We've kept you long enough. Thank you for your time and your generous hospitality. We can see ourselves out."

Birdie and Mamie said goodbye as well. None of us spoke another word until we were back in the crawler.

I started the vehicle and got us headed back to the factory. "Mamie, did you know she has two other children?"

She shook her head slowly. "I guess I did, but it's been so long since I've thought about them. I've been thinking George was an only child, honestly."

"He kind of is," Birdie said. "If his brother and sister don't live in the North Pole."

"True." I stopped at a red light. "No wonder Finnoula wanted to protect him so desperately. With her husband gone, George is all she has left."

Mamie frowned. "I take back everything I said or thought about her faking that illness."

"You had no way of knowing," Birdie said.

She shook her head like she was disgusted with herself. "Can you imagine the prospect of having your son about to be married, the promise of a new daughter-in-law, the possibility of grandchildren, all of that happiness? Then it's dashed, and you're left watching your son crumble? What a horrible thing. Especially on top of her knowing how sick she was."

The light went green, and I drove on. "I was thinking about that. How hard it must have been for her to realize the only way to save her son from one heartbreak was to tell him about another one. I feel for her. I feel for both of them."

Birdie's mouth pursed. "I don't mean to be insensitive—they've certainly had a hard time of things, Finnoula especially—but none of what we learned today explains why the hangar tours were stopped."

I sighed. "I was going to ask, but the moment slipped away."

Mamie shrugged. "Maybe they weren't stopped so much as they weren't renewed or something like that. It could have just been paperwork that got lost in the cracks during that time. I'm sure work wasn't his focus then."

"That's true," I said. "Or there's another reason we don't know about."

"I'll dig into it," Mamie said. "Finnoula probably doesn't know anyway. But I can check the records. If there's any kind of paper trail, I'll find it."

Birdie grinned. "You really are the North Pole equivalent of me."

Mamie's eyes twinkled. "Considering I'm your senior by about thirty years, I'd say it's the other way around."

We were still laughing as I parked in the factory lot. I thought Birdie liked being considered a younger woman, although I didn't think Mamie was quite thirty years older.

Winter elves aged very slowly and lived for a long, long time. About midlife, our physical aging slowed down, too, meaning I'd look like I was in my thirties for several more decades. No complaints from me.

"This was an interesting outing. I'm glad I got to see Finnoula. I need to visit her more often," Mamie said. She made no move to get out. I thought she'd enjoyed our little adventure. "I'll look into that hangar shutdown some more and see what I can come up with."

"Good. I can't wait to hear what you find out."

Birdie leaned up from the back seat. "What are we going to do next?"

My answer should probably have something to do with wedding stuff, but I wasn't quite ready to fall down that hole just yet. I turned to see Birdie in the back seat. "I was thinking we'd go see George at his office. Talk to him about reopening the hangar for tours."

She nodded. "Okay. Do you think Finnoula called him and told him we came by? And what you wanted to speak to him about?"

"She might have."

"I don't know," Mamie said. "She might not have. After all, if she told him that we stayed to talk, he might ask what we talked about. She definitely doesn't want to bring up anything that could upset him."

"Right." Finnoula had made that clear. "But since you two are old friends, she could just say you reminisced and leave it at that."

"Possibly." Mamie seemed unconvinced.

"Hmm." I narrowed my eyes, thinking of a new possibility.

"What is it?" Birdie asked.

"Do you think Finnoula's afraid of George? I mean, maybe this dark place he went to after Rachel left him, maybe it wasn't depression so much as rage."

Birdie and Mamie didn't answer right away, just sat there looking at me, considering what I'd just said.

Then Birdie sat back, arms crossed. "That's an interesting possibility."

Mamie put her hand to her chin. "You don't think the reason she hasn't been out is because he won't let her leave, do you? What if Rachel's leaving him really twisted him up to the point that he's afraid his mother might leave him too? Or that her going out might make her illness worse, meaning she'd pass away sooner? It's possible that all of that pain he went through has messed with his mind. Made him capable of doing terrible things."

Birdie made a raspberry. "Lots of men get dumped. They don't go psycho because of it. If that's what pushed him over the edge, he already had problems. Obviously."

We were all silent. All undoubtedly thinking about the bones in the carriage.

Mamie finally sighed. "We really don't know any more now than we did earlier, do we?"

"We do some," I said. "But it's brought up new questions as well."

"That's always how it is," Birdie added. "Takes a lot of digging to get to the truth."

I tapped my fingers on the console. "Yeah, and we still don't know who the skeleton belongs to."

"Do you think..." Birdie went quiet, leaving her sentence hanging.

I finished it for her. "That our skeleton is Rachel? I don't know."

The idea made me sick to my stomach. But once again, the thought that George might have killed her for leaving him popped into my head.

"We're getting ahead of ourselves," Mamie said. "Why don't you let me try to locate her? And when I do, I can get her side of the story. That should answer a lot of our questions."

"Good thinking," Birdie said. "That's much better than us speculating. Do you remember her last name?"

"Not off the top of my head. I seem to recall it was something unusual." Mamie smiled at her. "But I'll come up with it. That's what we do."

Birdie grinned right back. "It sure is. Let me know if I can help. I'm pretty handy with that kind of research."

"Will do. And you two keep me posted on your visit to George's. Time for me to get back to work."

My phone vibrated with an incoming message. I gave the screen a glance. "Hmm. That meeting with George will have to be postponed. LeRoy wants me to come by the shop and look at his new wedding dress design and give my input." I looked at Birdie. "Are you up for a trip to the royal couturier?"

Birdie was practically salivating. "To look at your wedding dress? Are you kidding? Of course I'm up for it. Let's go."

Mamie laughed as she got out. "Sounds like fun. I hope the dress is everything you dreamed of."

"Thanks, Mamie. Have a great day. We'll talk to you soon."

She waved goodbye and walked toward the factory entrance, badge in hand. Birdie climbed into the front seat, and we were off.

Birdie rubbed her hands together. "I can't wait to see the dress."

"Me either, especially after the last one." I shuddered.

"That bad?"

"Oh, Birdie, that dress is what caused my breakdown. It was a total nightmare. Or a train wreck. Whatever you want to call it. LeRoy is a sweet man, and I love him dearly, but you'd think for a designer of his clout, he'd have enough backbone to stand up to my mother and aunt. Then again, they are the queen and Mrs. Kringle, so I can't be too hard on him. But wow, it was next-level bad."

"I'm bummed I missed it."

"Settle down." I laughed. "I'm kind of bummed you missed it too. I think you could have talked some sense into my mom and aunt right there."

She shrugged. "I don't know. I might be an outspoken person, but I've never given a queen a piece of my mind."

"I suppose it's kind of intimidating if you think about it too much."

"Hey." She dug into her purse and pulled out the scrap of fabric she'd found under the skeleton.

"Do you think I could ask LeRoy about this? Fabric is kind of his specialty."

"Not only could you, I think you should. Especially because of how fancy it is. That's a great idea."

"Thanks." She tucked it away again. "We'll get all the wedding dress stuff out of the way first. That's the most important. Then we'll show him the fabric. That is, if you think he can be trusted."

"Of course. He's been the couturier for ages. He made my christening gown, you know. My mom's and aunt's gowns for most things. He makes all my uncle's suits too. He's a very talented man. And very sweet. You'll see."

We arrived a few minutes later. His shop was near the town square but set back on a small lane with a few other high-end retailers. I parked the crawler at the curb, and we headed inside.

"LeRoy?" I called out. "It's Jayne. We're here."

Birdie leaned in. "This shop is amazing. Do you think it would be okay if I took some pictures for Corette?"

"I want to say yes, but we'd better ask LeRoy."

"Ask me what, Your Highness?" He came from the back room, bowed, and gave me a big smile.

"Hi, LeRoy. This is my friend Birdie Caruthers. She's helping me with some wedding things while she's up here visiting from Nocturne Falls. One of our other friends there, Corette Williams, owns the bridal salon, and Birdie was wondering if she could take some pictures of your beautiful shop to show Corette."

Birdie nodded. "She would just love to see them, I know it. Your shop is so elegant. And to see the salon of the royal couturier would just be such a treat for her."

The sparkle in LeRoy's eyes gave away how tickled he was by the praise. "If seeing my shop would please her, then by all means, take some photos. And thank you for your kind words. I work very hard at what I do. It's always nice to be appreciated."

"Thank you," Birdie said. "That's very kind of you to allow the photos. But I know there's more important business to attend to first."

His smile broadened, and he rubbed his hands together. "Ah, yes. The gown." He gestured toward the rear of the store where the fitting rooms were, the largest of them the grand salon. "Ladies, if you would follow me, I would be happy to show you what I've been working on."

He took us back to the grand salon, and there on the riser in front of the mirrors was a dress form wearing a wedding gown. *My* wedding gown.

A little gasp came out of me. The dress was stunningly beautiful. I walked around it to take it all in. Sleek and body-hugging with a gentle V-neck in the front that was mimicked in the back with a deeper V. The train was maybe six feet or so and subtly beaded with crystal snowflakes, which was the dress's only adornment. But the fabric was what had caused me to gasp.

At first, I'd thought the dress was white, and I guess it was technically, but it shimmered glacial blue. I'd never seen anything like it, but based on some of the gowns I'd had, I also knew elf technology with fabric was pretty amazing.

I walked around the dress one more time, admiring it and watching the color play over it. I stopped when I reached LeRoy and Birdie.

His brows were raised in expectation.

I shook my head. "I don't think I've ever loved a dress more. You outdid yourself. This is nothing short of amazing. This fabric is just..." I sighed a happy sigh. "I love it. So much."

He exhaled. "I am so glad. I had this fabric made for you after the last dress went so terribly wrong. I knew you wanted simple, but at the same time, there is a certain expectation for a royal wedding gown."

Birdie nodded, but her eyes were on the dress. "It's amazing," she whispered.

With a gentle smile, LeRoy continued. "A royal wedding gown must look royal. It must be something special. Something people will talk about. Something that other brides will aspire to. But it must also reflect the personality of the bride."

He glanced at his creation, pride shining in his gaze. "I hope this is the dress that I have given you."

"You have. Absolutely." I pressed my hands together. "Can I try it on?" I looked at Birdie. "You don't mind, do you?"

"I'd be mad if you didn't. But shouldn't your mother be here for this?"

I bit my lip. "Good point." I really wanted her here too.

LeRoy cleared his throat. "I don't disagree, but a quick fitting would be very helpful. Then I could make some adjustments, and we'd be able to show your mother a much more finished version with the veil."

"What does the veil look like?" I asked.

"For this dress, it will match the length of the train. The top will attach to your tiara, then fall unadorned to midback, where a building cascade of hand-beaded snowflakes will drift to the bottom."

Birdie sighed. "It sounds lovely."

"It does," I agreed. "Okay, a quick fitting, but just so my mom and aunt don't feel left out, I don't think you should see me in it, Birdie. Not until they get to."

"Absolutely. While you do that, I'll go take some pictures of the salon."

"Perfect. Thank you for understanding."

"Of course."

LeRoy gestured toward the back of the store. "Charlotte is in the storeroom. I'll get her, and she can help you into the dress. If you'll excuse me."

He left us, and Birdie sighed again. "You're going to look so beautiful in that dress. I bet Sinclair cries."

I laughed. "I don't know about that."

"I do. Look at that thing. You're going to float down the aisle in all that silk like a fairy princess. Which you pretty much are." She shook her head. "It's going to be amazing."

"I think so too."

LeRoy and Charlotte came back in.

Birdie gave me a wink. "Enjoy your fitting. I'll be out in the salon taking pictures."

"Thanks."

The fitting was quick, mostly because I suddenly wanted the dress done so I could show it to my mom, my aunt, and Birdie all at once. I knew they'd love it. At least, I hoped they would. *They* being my mom and aunt. This dress had none of the flourishes and embellishments they'd added to the first one, but I thought they'd understand.

If not, Birdie was here to gently guide them to my way of seeing things.

Once I was back in the fitting room to change, I slipped my phone out of my purse and snapped a pic of myself in the mirror. The dress was so beautiful, I wanted to be able to look at it whenever I liked.

Then I sent Sin a quick text. *Tried my new wedding dress on. So much better. Hope your day is going well.* I finished it with a heart.

After that, I got back into my street clothes, said goodbye to LeRoy, and went to find Birdie. I almost ran into her coming back to the fitting rooms. Her eyes were wide with excitement, and she was practically quivering.

"What's up? Did you ask LeRoy about the fabric? Or do you want me to?"

She shook her head and whispered, "Later."

"Okay, what then?"

"We should go. Now."

This was getting weird. What on earth could have gotten her wound up like this? I turned and called out, "Thanks again, LeRoy. Love the dress. See you soon."

"Thanks," Birdie added. "Lovely shop, great dress, nice to meet you."

We were out the door a second later, with Birdie almost herding me toward the crawler. We got in, got our seat belts on, and then I couldn't wait any longer.

"What gives?"

"Look." She pulled out her phone and showed me a picture of LeRoy's rogues' gallery. It was the little hallway between the main shop area and the fitting rooms. The walls were lined with photos of all the people he'd dressed in the clothes he'd made for them. My parents and aunt and uncle were on there quite a bit, but the gallery featured all kinds of local celebrities, dignitaries, and political folks.

LeRoy might be the royal couturier, but if someone had the money, and LeRoy had the time, he'd make an outfit for anyone. Well, anyone who could finagle an appointment. LeRoy was booked up months and months in advance.

Mostly, he dressed women, but he did make my uncle's suits. He'd also made my father's coronation cape. But it was women who flocked to him. He had a talent with design that did wonderful things for a woman's figure.

I shrugged. "I don't know what I'm looking at."

"This woman." She used two fingers to make the screen bigger, zooming in.

"That's one of the NP's former mayors, the Honorable Pinneta Greene. She was the mayor when I was born." That was a big part of why I knew who she was. "She serves on the Royal Historical Society board now."

"Okay, great, but look closer."

I stared at the picture for a moment, then realized what I was seeing. My mouth came open. "Son of a nutcracker. Her dress."

Birdie nodded. "The fabric matches the scrap I found under the skeleton."

Birdie and I stared at the photo for one more second, then we looked at each other.

The weight of this discovery pressed down on me so hard I could feel it in my bones. "We have to tell the constable about this."

She nodded. "I agree. It's too important a clue for us to keep to ourselves. We can still investigate it, though. But who do you think it implicates? The mayor? Or..."

She didn't have to finish the sentence.

"No." I sighed with all the heaviness that was suddenly on my heart. "This points to LeRoy. But it can't be him. It just can't be. He's not the murdering type. You've met him. Do you think he's capable of harming someone?"

"No, but are you saying the mayor is?"

"No. But I also don't know her as well. So... maybe? But that's a crazy thing to assume about anyone." I leaned back in the driver's seat and stared skyward. "All this really tells us is that LeRoy might be tied to this somehow."

"I don't think we can rule the mayor out, though. Not when she's wearing a dress in this picture that's made of the same fabric I found under the bones."

"Granted." I groaned. "This is insane. We need to know who that skeleton is."

"Then let's go see the constable. Or the ME. Or both. Maybe they know something more. We have to tell the constable about this new development anyway."

"Or..." I took a breath, not sure I believed what I was about to say. "We could tell the constable what we've found, then let her handle this and go back to working on the wedding prep like we're supposed to be."

Birdie squinted at me, then reached over and put her hand on my forehead.

"What are you doing?"

"Checking to see if you have a fever. The Jayne I know would never suggest a thing like that."

"I feel fine. I just can't imagine that LeRoy is involved in this. He's a good man. He can't be a part of this. I don't want to find out differently."

"Then let's prove him innocent."

I turned toward her slightly. "But what if he isn't?"

"Wouldn't you rather know?"

"That's what I'm saying. I'm genuinely not sure."

"That really doesn't sound like the Jayne I know. What gives?"

I hesitated, then took a breath. "I'm ashamed to say this, but it's the dress."

"What?"

I chewed on the inside of my cheek, glad this was Birdie I was talking to and not someone who would judge me. "I love that wedding dress. It's beautiful. It's everything I ever wanted in a wedding gown and a few things I didn't know I wanted but do now. And if LeRoy is guilty of murder—if he's even guilty of being an accessory to murder—I won't be able to wear it. Royal protocol wouldn't allow it. The scandal would be too much. The royal family can't be associated with that kind of thing."

"Of course not," Birdie said. Her brows knit together. "It would be a terrible shame to give that dress up."

"And the thought of having to get another dress designed, of going through that again..." I shook my head. "I think I'd crack for real."

"Do you think he *could* be involved?"

I gave my answer a lot of honest thought. "No. I really don't. But I also know people are capable of just about anything if put into a difficult enough position."

She pursed her lips. "We really only have one option."

"I know." I put my metaphorical big-girl panties on. "We have to find out who's really to blame."

I drove us straight to the constable's office. Thankfully, she was there, even though it was approaching dinnertime. She came out of her office with an uncertain expression. No doubt wondering if I was there to check up on her progress.

Which I guess I was. But that wasn't the main reason Birdie and I had come. "Hi. We don't want to interrupt you, but we have some information to share."

Her expression softened into one of curiosity. "Come into my office, then."

We did, closing the door behind us. Birdie dug into her pocket and took out the scrap of fabric. "I found this in the carriage right after I found the skeleton. It was under the right foot. I know how wrong it was of me to take it, and I'm sorry."

The constable frowned. "You of all people should know better."

"And I do. I don't know what came over me. But there's more, and I hope the new information will help you overlook my indiscretion."

"Birdie didn't mean any harm," I said. "She just thought she ought to tell me about the fabric first. Seeing as how I'm the princess and all." I hated throwing my royal weight around like that, but I didn't want Birdie to get into trouble.

Especially since I was pretty sure the constable could charge her with evidence tampering or some such.

With a stern look, Larsen leaned back in her chair. "Yes, well, I'll reserve judgment until I see what this new information is."

I nudged Birdie. "Go on. Show her."

Birdie pulled her phone out. "We were just at LeRoy's bridal shop—"

"I had a fitting for my wedding gown." Not that the constable couldn't figure that out, but reminding her about the wedding might soften her toward Birdie a little. It was worth a shot anyway.

Birdie sucked in a breath and put her hand to her chest. "The most gorgeous gown you've ever seen. Anyway, I was taking some photos of the shop for a friend back home—with LeRoy's permission—and upon closer inspection, I found this."

She turned the phone around so the photo of the former mayor was on display.

Constable Lawson narrowed her eyes. Then leaned in. "Is that the same fabric?"

"We think it is." I shook my head. "I don't know much about Pinneta Greene, other than she's long retired. But I do know LeRoy. I've known him all my life. So has my mother and my aunt and—"

"I'm well aware of his connection to your family," the constable interrupted.

I didn't appreciate the interruption. And it was an out-of-character thing for her to do. Not just because it was rude, but it was also impolite to interrupt a royal. Was she mad at us for what Birdie had done? Or was something else going on? I planned to find out. "I'm just saying that he's not the type of man who'd be involved in something like this."

When she didn't say anything right away, I leaped on the opportunity to dig deeper. "What's got you upset, Constable? Because something is clearly bothering you."

She sighed. "The ME's early findings show that the cause of death was definitely murder. She was stabbed to death. Now, bear in mind he's not done with his examination. Not by a long shot. But marks on the ribs indicate a slim, pointed object was used. Blunt on one side, sharpened on the other."

I shrugged. "That could be any kind of knife."

She glanced at the paperwork on her desk, which I realized had the ME's seal at the top. The rest of the writing was too small and too upside down for me to make out anything useful. "Dr. Charming doesn't think it was a knife."

"Then what?" Birdie asked.

"Scissors." The constable's stern expression

returned. "Could be like those used in dressmaking."

I went numb. Could LeRoy really be involved in this? I was out of words, and my heart ached.

Birdie seemed to understand that I needed to leave. She got us out of there with a thank-you and a quick goodbye.

I was still numb an hour later as I stood staring out my apartment window into the gardens. Twilight had fallen, but the moonlight sparkled on the snowy ground. It was beautiful. Not that any of it was really registering.

Birdie was in the kitchen, fixing me a cup of tea, which I didn't want, but she insisted would help.

"It can't be him," I muttered for the umpteenth time.

"It's not," Birdie answered from the kitchen.

"He's a good man. A kind man. He's not a murderer."

"No, he's not," she said. "Even I can tell that after our brief introduction."

I sighed and closed my eyes as I leaned against the window frame. "And I feel terrible about how concerned I am over the dress. I'm a shallow, selfish person."

"No, you're not. You're a bride on the brink of a breakdown. You get a little leeway for that. Now go sit on the couch before you faint away."

"I'm fine." But I sat on the couch anyway.

Spider jumped up beside me. "Mama sad."

I petted his soft head. "Yes, baby, I am."

Birdie came over with the tea, which was peppermint and smelled wonderful. "I still can't get over that your cat talks, but it's nice you have such a wise little man to keep you company." She put the tea on the coffee table, then sat across from me.

"Sin's cat can talk, too, thanks to a translation collar one of my uncle's tinkers designed."

Birdie's brows lifted. "How about that."

I picked up the cup and took a sip. She'd added a lot of sugar. I took another sip. She was right, the tea was making me feel better. "I can't tell my mom and aunt about this. They'll be heartbroken."

"Well, the constable agreed to keep everything under wraps for as long as possible, so that should help. So did Ezreal. And Larsen said she'd call as soon as she got more from the ME." Birdie had gone to see Ezreal to fill him in as soon as we got back. "In the meantime, we need to figure out who our dead woman is and what connection, if any, she might have to LeRoy."

I nodded and drank a little more tea. "We should have told the constable about Rachel."

"We still can. Or I can. Do you want me to go see her?"

I shook my head. "Tomorrow. We need to eat dinner. Or I might just go to bed."

Spider flopped down next to me and tipped his head over my leg, looking at me upside down.

The utter cuteness of him made me smile. "Silly boy."

"Spider love Mama."

He was trying to cheer me up and doing a pretty good job of it. "I love you too, baby."

A knock sounded at the door, then it opened. Sin walked in, his handsome face a welcome sight. "Honey, I'm home. Are you ready for dinner?" Then his smile vanished. "Are you all right?"

"I'm…okay. How was class?"

"It was fine, and you are not okay. I can tell that just by looking at you."

A little half smile was all I could muster. "Birdie can bring you up to speed."

He joined me on the couch as she did just that, showing him the photo of the former mayor on her phone and pointing out the fabric. "The plot thickens," he said.

I nodded. "That's for sure."

He sat back, quiet for a moment. "What do you say we put all of this away for the evening and go eat some pizza? Or something really comforting? Whatever you want, sweetheart."

I knew he was trying to make me feel better. And it was working, a little. "Pizza would be nice."

"Do you want to eat it here? Or the dining room?"

Thinking about something else was already making me feel better. "How about we have some pizzas sent up here and watch a movie?"

Birdie nodded. "I love that idea."

"Then it's settled."

Sin went to the phone. "What kind of pizzas do we want? The kitchen can make anything, right?"

"Right." I glanced at Birdie. "Meat lovers?"

She nodded. "That's me."

I looked at Sin. "Meat lovers and whatever you want. I'll eat anything."

"You got it." He dialed and ordered the pies, including a plain cheese and one with ham and mushrooms. I also heard him order chocolate cake. When he hung up, he gave me a nod. "Twenty minutes."

We spent the rest of the night eating and watching a comedy. I couldn't really forget about everything else that was going on, but the food and the movie and the company helped.

At least until the next morning.

After how relaxed we'd been the previous night, Sin had decided we should stay in for breakfast as well, so he'd called the kitchen and ordered breakfast for the three of us delivered to my apartment. Not having to dress and go down to breakfast was a treat. Even Birdie showed up in her robe and slippers.

It was the perfect low-stress way to start the day. Except for the part where someone in the kitchen wrote down the delivery time wrong.

Because of that, we were settled around the table being served our omelets and pancakes when most of the palace was probably still in bed.

The footman in charge of the delivery apologized repeatedly until I held my hand up. "It's all right. Mistakes happen. An early start isn't such a bad thing." I was trying to look on the bright side. "We'll get more done today."

He nodded. "Thank you, Your Highness."

He left and we all went for our coffee. Once we'd downed a bit of that, we started to eat. The food was good, even if I wasn't truly awake enough to appreciate it.

Near the end of the meal, the apartment phone rang.

Sin got up. "I'll get it."

"Probably my mom wondering why we didn't come down for breakfast."

"No," Sin said. "I sent them a note that we were eating in."

"Thanks, that was nice of you." I drank some more coffee and scratched the belly of Spider, who was curled up on the kitchen chair beside me. I listened to see if the constable was on the phone. The weight of the unsolved murder pressed on me. I just wanted this case cracked so we could put it behind us.

Sin held the phone to his chest. "Sweetheart, it's Mamie. She wants to speak to you."

"Okay." I gave Spider one last scratch and got up, taking the phone from Sin. "Mamie? It's Jayne."

"Hi, Jayne. Sorry to call so early, but I did the digging you asked, and I have some news."

"No worries, we're all up anyway."

"Perfect. There's no record of George's ex currently living in the North Pole. In fact, as far as I can tell, there's no record of the woman having *ever* lived in the North Pole."

"That's odd."

"I know, right? But wait, there's more. I remembered what her last name was, obviously, since I needed it for the search."

"And?" This had to be good, or Mamie wouldn't have saved it for last.

She took a breath. "It's Brightmoore."

The surname processed in an instant. "That's not a winter elf name."

"No, it's not."

"But that pretty much explains why there'd be no record of her living here. With a name like that, she has to be a summer elf."

"Yes," Mamie confirmed. "That's what I was thinking too. I hope that helps."

"It certainly explains some things. Like the engagement ring. George said Rachel was his sun. Now we know just how true that was. Thank you."

"You're welcome. Have a good day."

"You too." I hung up and went back to the table.

"Well, now," Birdie said as I sat down. "Did I hear right? George's ex is a summer elf? Isn't your ex Cooper a summer elf?"

I nodded. "He is, yes."

Sin looked a little confused. "What's interesting about it?"

Birdie lifted one shoulder. "A summer elf and a winter elf engaged to be married? It's at least curious."

"I guess." He didn't seem convinced. He refilled his coffee from the carafe on the table. "How many summer elves live in the NP?"

"I'm sure there are some, but it's not like we have a registry of them or anything," I said. My pumpkin, white chocolate chip pancakes were almost gone, making me a little sad. "I'm guessing not many, though."

He nodded. "I see. So it would be a little out of the ordinary for them to be engaged, let alone meet."

"Yes. Winter elves do marry other kinds of supernaturals. You and I are proof of that. But winter elves who marry summer elves don't usually make their home in the NP. Summer elves just can't handle the cold here. Most of them choose to live in the Southern parts of the mortal world." One more reason Cooper and I wouldn't have worked out.

Birdie shifted back in her chair, a slice of bacon in one hand. "Then how would George have met Rachel, do you think?"

"Well, Finnoula did say her other two children live in the mortal world. Maybe he met her visiting them. Or maybe the same way I met Cooper. In college."

Sin added more syrup to his remaining pancakes. He'd gotten blueberry buttermilk. "You know, I bet Finnoula would have liked Rachel and the possibility of moving out of the NP with her son and new daughter-in-law."

"You think so? Why?" I couldn't imagine a woman as set in her life as Finnoula wanting to move.

"Because, according to the research I did, warmer climates can greatly alleviate the symptoms of Grater's."

That was new information. "Really? When on earth did you have time to research that? Did you figure out a way to clone yourself? If so, I want in."

He grinned. "The class instructor is a very knowledgeable man. And he's pretty easy to get off track. One question and off he goes. Apparently, his grandfather was a miner, contracted Grater's, and moved to Florida for his retirement, where he's doing much better. On a side note, I didn't learn very much about royal life yesterday."

I snorted. "I still think your time was well spent. That's a pretty interesting fact. And it adds new questions to the mix. We still don't know why George and Rachel broke up, or why George canceled the hangar tours, but now I'd also like to know if someone had a reason to keep Finnoula from moving out of the North Pole with George and Rachel after they were married. Or a reason to keep George from moving. If so, who would want to do that?"

Birdie sighed. "I also think we need to see if LeRoy has any connection to the Bitterbarks."

Sadly, I knew she was right. "I know. And I think we should start with LeRoy. Just flat out ask him if he knows them and how. Go straight to the source, right?"

"Right." She stared at me a little more intently. "Are you up for that this morning?"

I was. "Yes. There's no point in putting it off. The longer this goes on, the harder it is. Of course, his shop doesn't open for three more hours, so we'll have to put it off a little bit."

The phone rang again, sending Sin to his feet. "I'll get it."

He answered, "Princess Jayne's apartment." He nodded. "I'll let her know, thank you."

"Let me know what?"

He hung up and looked at me. "Apparently, we have a cake tasting at White's Fine Pastries in an hour. That was them confirming. I'd better call and let my instructor know I won't be in class this morning."

"We have a cake tasting at eight A.M.?" I slapped my forehead as the appointment came back to me. "Ugh. We do. Good thing the kitchen messed up the time for our breakfast or I'd still be in bed."

Birdie frowned. "That appointment's not in the binder. You didn't tell me about that."

"Because I didn't remember until just now." I shook my head. "We have to go. Canceling will mean the shop's hard work and cake go to waste. I'm not doing that to the bakers."

"Do you want me to talk to LeRoy, then?" Birdie asked. "I can work on wedding things until his shop opens."

"No, I want you with us. We might need a tiebreaker, so having a third taster will be perfect."

Sin nodded. "I agree. Come with us. Helping us with the wedding decisions was the whole reason we asked you here. Plus...cake."

She smiled. "You don't have to twist my arm. But I'd better go get ready."

"We all need to," I said. "Back here in forty?"

"Done," Sin said.

White's was the oldest bakery in the NP and had baked my mother's wedding cake, which was why I wanted to use them. The royal kitchens could have made the cake, but traditionally that was hired out because they were already in charge of the wedding dinner. There was no point in burdening them unduly.

Plus, it was a real feather in the shop's cap to do a royal event. As a family, we liked to help the local businesses whenever we could. Not that White's needed the business, I suppose, but I knew a new generation had just taken over.

Baking our wedding cake would be our way of giving support to this new generation.

Julianne White, the great-great-granddaughter of

Earnest White, the shop's founder, greeted us with a quick curtsy as we walked in. "It's a pleasure to have you here today, Princess and Consort."

"Thank you," I answered. "It's a pleasure to be here."

Sin thanked her as well, then gestured toward Birdie. "This is our friend Birdie Caruthers. She's helping us with some wedding things. I realize you haven't prepared for three of us today, but I hope that's all right."

"Oh, it's just fine." Julianne smoothed her snowy apron. "There's plenty of cake for tasting."

Birdie sighed with happiness. "Such good news."

With a laugh, Julianne directed us to a small table set up in the back room of the bakery. Several other bakers were working at their stations. Two were decorating cakes, and one was scooping cookie dough onto baking sheets. Another was carrying enormous bags of flour. The place smelled of vanilla and batter and yeasty goodness.

I inhaled and let the delicious aromas put me in the right frame of mind. Tasting cakes might not be the most important thing I could be doing right now, but it certainly wasn't going to be a hardship. Everything else could wait. Especially the skeleton that had already waited some thirty years.

Besides, the constable was on the case.

"Please," Julianne said. "Have a seat, and I'll bring the first selection of samples over."

The small table had four chairs, so we each took a spot while she went to one of the baking racks near the ovens.

She brought over a tray with multiple slices of cake on it, along with some small plates, forks, knives, and serving utensils. She put a setting in front of each of us, then sat. "All right, let me tell you what we have for round one, and then I'll serve."

She pointed to the slices as she spoke. "This one is winterberry jam with white chocolate frosting and French vanilla chiffon cake. Very popular with brides getting married around the holiday season, although I know your wedding isn't until February."

I nodded. "We couldn't overlap with Christmas. That's already such a crazy time of year for my family."

"Totally understand," Julianne said. "Next is a chocolate ganache with marzipan filling and an orange essence sponge. I do more of this in the fall, but the flavor combination is delicious any time of year. Lastly on this tray is an eggnog fudge buttercream with spice cake. The eggnog fudge is, of course, a nod to your aunt's famous confection."

Birdie raised her hand.

Julianne grinned. "Yes?"

"If this is round one, how many rounds are there?"

"Three. With three samples in each one."

Birdie's grin was wide and infectious. She looked at Sin and me and shook her head. "How are you two ever going to decide?"

Sin snorted. "I told you we were going to need you."

"Not sure how much help I'll be. I already love them all." She picked up a fork. "But let's put them to the real test."

Julianne served us, then we happily dug in. We thoroughly enjoyed them all. I voted against the eggnog, however, because as delicious as it was, I knew there would be eggnog fudge on the dessert trays being passed, so there was no point in doubling up.

We also nixed the winterberry. It was one of my mother's favorites, but the strong mint flavor was off-putting to some. Winterberry was a love-it-or-hate-it kind of flavor. The chocolate and orange, always a delicious combination, was put on the list of possibilities.

Round two brought a traditional fruitcake with cream cheese frosting, a tuxedo cake of dark chocolate with vanilla cream mousse, and cappuccino cake with a mocha ganache.

We all agreed that the cappuccino cake was outstanding. That went on the possibles list as well. The fruitcake felt too Christmasy, and the tuxedo cake was outstanding, but we thought our wedding cake should be something more unique.

Julianne brought the third and final round to us with a real sparkle in her eyes. "These three are the most special of the bunch, which is why I saved them for last."

"What makes them so special?" Birdie asked.

I could always count on her to say what I was thinking.

"Because," Julianne said, "two of them are custom flavors."

She set the tray down, and before she could describe them, Sin pointed to the one in the middle. "That smells like a glazed doughnut."

She nodded. "Excellent. That's what I was going for. It's a yeast cake with a sugar glaze and a pastry cream filling." She cut the slice into three pieces and put it on our plates. "Taste it and tell me what you think."

We did. Happy noises came out of all of us.

Sin's lasted a little longer. "That is amazing. It's a glazed and filled doughnut, no doubt about it." He put his fork down and looked at me. "We don't have to have that for the wedding cake, but I at least want that for the groom's cake."

"Done," I said. I turned to Julianne. "Could we have it as one of the wedding cake layers? Nothing says all the layers have to be the same, right?"

Julianne nodded. "That's right. They don't have to be. You can alternate them however you like. People do it all the time. Although for the best-looking cake, the exterior frosting needs to be consistent."

Sin looked at me. "You wouldn't mind having different layers?"

"Not at all. This glazed-doughnut cake is a great tribute to who you are. We kind of met because of doughnuts. Why shouldn't it be part of the wedding cake?"

He looked unconvinced. "A glazed-doughnut cake doesn't sound very royal."

"Who cares what sounds royal? This cake is about us." I put my hand on his and looked at Julianne. I would fight the royal etiquette committee for this one. "The glazed-doughnut cake is in. What's next?"

She started serving up the slice on the right. It had a slightly pink filling with dark red cake and looked like strawberry or raspberry to me. "This one has a vanilla buttercream exterior with Dr Pepper buttercream filling and Dr Pepper velvet cake."

My mouth fell open. "Are you serious?"

I didn't wait for her answer, just forked up a mouthful and inhaled it. Pure happiness spilled through me at the complete and utter Dr Pepper sugar explosion going on in my mouth. I started nodding. "I want this," I mumbled around crumbs and buttercream. "No, I *need* this."

Then I pointed my fork at the sample as I looked at Sin and Birdie. "You guys. Taste it already."

They did, nodding immediately. Sin laughed softly. "That might be the most Jayne cake ever created."

Julianne's grin widened. "I was really hoping you'd like that one."

I swallowed my third bite of the confection. "Like it? I love it! I'm not sure I even want to taste the last one."

"Oh," Julianne said, "I really think you should. It's our royal vanilla. Vanilla buttercream with vanilla mousse filling with vanilla cake. I know that doesn't sound very exciting, but it's all made with our special vanilla-infused sugar and flour. And the cake also has vanilla beans from fresh pods and vanilla syrup."

She was right. It sounded nice, but not all that exciting. I wanted to be polite, though. "Why is it called royal vanilla?"

"Because," she said with a smile, "it's the wedding cake White's baked for your mother and father. It was created especially for them by my great-grandpa Earnest."

My heart squeezed a little, and Birdie put her hand to her cheek.

Sin picked up his fork. "We absolutely need to taste it."

Julianne's eyes sparkled as she served us. Clearly, she was proud of this cake. I couldn't wait to try it.

So we did. And it was divine. Vanilla, yes, but

such a complex layered vanilla experience that it made vanilla taste new.

"Amazing," Sin said. "That would make an incredible cake doughnut."

Birdie shook her head, still chewing. "I didn't know vanilla could taste like this."

Julianne nodded. "It's the layering of the vanilla that does it. My great-grandfather worked very hard on the recipe. But that's not the only reason it's a very special cake. The vanilla sugar alone takes six months to properly infuse."

Sin took my hand. "Let's have all three. What do you say?"

Happiness filled me. "Yes. That's perfect. That's exactly what I want too."

Birdie clapped softly. "I love it. A nod to both of you and your parents." Then she tipped her head to one side and gave Sin a curious look. "Sinclair, I can't help but ask...what about your parents?"

I turned toward him as well. "You know, Birdie's right. Every time I've asked you about your parents, you say they're traveling or in the midst of a project, and you immediately change the subject. Don't think I haven't noticed."

He looked guilty as charged.

"I assume you've told them we're getting married, but I haven't even met them. I really should before the wedding, don't you think?"

He swallowed. "Yes."

The tentative tone of that single word spoke volumes. He didn't want to discuss this here. Not in front of Julianne and her workers, anyway. I could understand that.

I focused my attention back on Julianne and gave her my princess smile. "Thank you for all the delicious samples today. I'm so glad we were able to decide on those three cakes. Let's do them in layers as you see fit, with the top tier being the royal vanilla."

"That sounds wonderful. We'll do the cake exactly like that, then. Now, as far as the design goes, I know you weren't completely happy about the sketches my artist sent over—"

"About that." I pulled Matilda's drawing from my purse. "This is how I'd like the cake to look."

Julianne took the drawing and studied it. Slowly, she smiled. "This is lovely. Extravagant, but still royal. We can certainly replicate this. May I ask...is this your design?"

"Oh, no, that was done by one of the citizens of the realm. A young girl named Matilda. I'd very much like it if you could include her somehow in the decorating? She wants to be a baker when she grows up, and I think, based on this design, that she could be one of the great ones. Maybe even work here someday."

Julianne nodded. "We do love to encourage new talent. Especially in the little ones."

"I'll have the palace steward send her information to you, then. And thank you again for today." I stood. "We'll be in touch."

Sin and Birdie said their goodbyes, then we left. The moment we got out to the crawler and shut the doors, I turned toward Sin. "Okay, explain. What's going on with your parents?"

He sighed in a way that didn't fill me with good feelings. "My parents are... That is..." He sighed again and shifted in his seat.

"Do you not want me to meet them?"

He frowned. "Is that an option?"

I stared at him. I was starting to get truly freaked out. "Is there something wrong with me? Do you think they won't like me? Do they have something against royals? What are you afraid of?"

"Jayne, you're the most perfect woman I've ever met. What I'm afraid of is that you'll meet my parents and..." He took a moment. The muscles in his jaw twitched. "You won't want to marry me. And that your parents will agree with you."

My jaw fell open. "Why on earth would you think that?"

"I am a *necromancer*."

"I know." But clearly, there was something I

didn't. "What does that have to do with your parents?"

He spoke softly and with great reluctance. "Do you know what it takes for a necromancer to be created? How someone with my abilities is created?"

I shook my head.

"I do," Birdie said.

Of course she did.

I glanced at her.

She shrugged. "You pick up a lot of interesting things in my line of work."

"Obviously," I said. "So what does it take?"

With the most innocent expression I'd ever seen, she said, "Well, either both his parents are necromancers…"

I glanced at Sin. "Are they?"

Sin shook his head. "They aren't."

I shot Birdie a look.

She made a little face that was in between sympathy and curiosity. "Then I'm pretty sure it requires one of his parents to be a zombie."

The loudest silence I'd ever heard filled the crawler. While it deafened me, I realized the name of Sin's doughnut shop—Zombie Donuts—not only made sense, but it was actually a sweet tribute to one of his parents.

Then Sinclair let out the most heart-wrenching groan. "I really screwed up."

A sudden burst of anxiety made me chew my lip. He was hurting, and I was hurting for him. I grabbed his arm, needing to connect with him. "No, you didn't. This is all fixable. But does that mean Birdie's right?"

He nodded, but his eyes were squeezed tight, and he was grimacing. "Yes."

"Which one of your parents is it?"

"My mother."

"Your mother is a zombie." I took my hand back as I tried to process that. The images that filled my head weren't great. But there was no closing this door now. With a gentle tone that I hoped was also filled with understanding, I ventured forth. "How…much of a zombie is she?"

His frown deepened. "You mean is she rotting away, or just slightly moldy?"

Yikes. "I wasn't—"

He put his hands up to stop me, his frown softening slightly. "You were, and that's okay. It's what everyone wants to know. I didn't mean to respond so sharply. It's just that…"

"She's your mom. Of course you're going to defend her. You wouldn't be the man I love if you didn't."

"Thanks." He took a breath, but it didn't seem to help. I'd never seen him look so deflated.

"What about your dad? He's not a zombie, then?"

"No. He's a conjurer. They've got a show in Vegas at the Oasis Resort. My mother is his assistant. It's quite an act. They've been headlining for years. Maybe you've heard of it. Dead Sexy." A strangled half sob, half laugh came out of Sin.

"Is that why you suggested we elope to Vegas? So I could meet them?"

"No. Just coincidence."

I grabbed his hand, still hurting for him. He was obviously very worried about all of this. "Hey, I don't care who or what your parents are, as long as they're decent people, which they have to be to have raised a son like you. Nothing is going to change how I feel about you. Nothing. We're getting married. That's definitely happening. Do you hear me?"

He nodded, still clearly unconvinced.

"Sin, I mean it."

"I know you do, and that's sweet, but I bet there are things going through your head right now that you don't even want to put into words."

"No, there aren't." There totally were. Like the images that had first come to me when he'd confirmed the zombie business. And what his gene pool meant for our future.

"Oh, really?" His gaze held a challenge. "So you're not wondering if one of our children could be a zombie?"

He'd read my mind. I gulped down my next breath, choking on it a little. "Is that…a possibility?"

He shook his head. "No. They'll be winter elf or some kind of magic-wielder or a mix of those two. There's always a slight chance one could be a necromancer, I suppose. But zombies are made, not born."

I sighed in relief before realizing what I'd done.

His frown returned instantly. "This is my fault. I should have told you sooner. I know that. I just couldn't."

"It's okay."

"No, it's not." He started the crawler. "If you want to break things off, I understand. And I'm very sorry."

"Sin, *stop* it." I put my hand on the wheel so he couldn't drive yet. "This changes nothing. Yes, you should have told me sooner, but why does it matter who your mother is? What on earth does that have to do with my love for you?"

He kept the crawler in park and turned toward me. "Jayne, there were people in this town who didn't think you should be involved with me because I'm a necromancer. Do you think the news about my mother is going to be met with open arms?"

"Those people were a minority. And one of them is under house arrest for the remainder of his life." Frankly, I was a little worked up. Maybe even borderline mad. "Now listen to me, Sinclair Crowe. Invite your parents up here immediately. I need to meet them. And they need to meet me. And my parents. Do you hear me? We're getting married, and we're not doing it without them."

He was still frowning, but the look in his eyes told me he was coming around. "You're opening a can of worms."

Birdie snorted, then stifled herself. "Whoops. Sorry. I thought that was a zombie joke."

Suddenly, I snorted too. It *was* funny. Sin looked like he was struggling to hold on to his frown.

Then his frown disappeared, and we were all laughing so hard we were crying.

At last, Sin took a big shuddering breath and shook his head. "I messed up."

"Yeah, you did. But who hasn't? And this is really fixable. We just need to meet each other." I smiled at him. I loved him so much. Nothing was going to change that. "Do they know you're getting married? Have you told them about me?"

"I have. They really want to meet you. But they also understand that they might not be every bride's dream in-laws."

"Oh, honey. I'm so sorry you've been carrying this around. But you should know me well enough to know that my love for you isn't conditional."

"I do know that." He took my hand and kissed my knuckles. "But you're also the heir to the Winter Throne. And after what we went through with Gregory..." He shrugged. "I let all of that get to me."

"I understand." Gregory, the former palace steward, had done his best to end Sinclair's chances with me. And my chances with the throne. "But no more, okay? I want to meet them. And they deserve to be a part of our lives. And part of our special day."

He kissed my hand again. "Thank you for being so understanding. I'll call them as soon as we get back to the palace." His eyes narrowed. "I can call them, can't I?"

"I'm not sure. We might have to talk to Ingvar about a special NP-to-Vegas connection. But we'll figure it out. Let's head home now. LeRoy's shop won't be open for another hour anyway."

When we returned to the palace, Birdie went to her apartment to add the cake selections to the wedding binder. Sin and I went to my dad's office to fill him in on Sin's parents. And as it turned out, Ingvar had already installed a landline that could reach numbers outside of the NP. Conveniently, that phone was on my dad's desk. There was also one in my uncle's office, but there was no point in going to the factory.

My dad and I left Sin alone to make the call. I figured he could use the privacy. Making a call like that with an audience, especially your future father-in-law, wouldn't be easy.

Besides, Mrs. Greenbaum had a fresh batch of lingonberry scones sitting on the filing cabinet. My dad and I each took one. How I had the room after breakfast and cake was proof of the sheer strength of the winter elf metabolism.

My dad didn't bite into his right away. "You know there could be some pushback about his mother."

"I know. I'm really hoping there's not, but I'm also not a complete Pollyanna. It wasn't that long ago a minority got worked up about me marrying a necromancer." I nibbled on the end of the scone.

Mrs. Greenbaum tsked. "People love to complain about anything just to hear the sound of their own voices. You ignore that. And those of us who truly love you will only care that you're happy."

"Thanks, Mrs. Greenbaum. But it's hard to ignore some of those complaints when you're the next-in-line ruler of those people."

"I'm sure it is, but you can't let those small minds interrupt your happiness or dictate how you live your life."

My dad nodded. "She's not wrong."

I wiped a crumb off my face. "No, she's not." I looked at her. "My future mother-in-law is a zombie."

Her eyes widened ever so slightly. "Oh?" She was silent for a moment, then she pursed her lips. "I don't see what it matters as long as she's a good, respectable person. For the record, there are already zombies living here, but their dead bits are all on the inside."

A slow smile turned up the corners of my mouth. "You're a gem, Mrs. Greenbaum. Thank you for that."

"You're welcome, Your Highness."

Sin opened the door of my dad's office. The phone was still to his ear. "Jack, can you give me the coordinates for the palace?"

"Sure. I'll jot them down for you." He went into the office with Sin.

While they were in there, the outer office door opened, and Ezreal came in. "There you are, Princess. The constable's looking for you. The ME has finished his preliminary report."

"Great, thank you." A little tingle of excitement rippled through me. "Does she want us to come by the station, or did she send the info here?"

"She wants you to come by." He nodded a quick greeting to Mrs. Greenbaum before speaking to me again. "And since we're talking about that case, I have to tell you I haven't uncovered any missing person that fits the timeline."

"That's okay. I appreciate you looking. Can you ring Constable Larsen back and tell her we'll be by in half an hour?"

"Will do."

"Thank you."

Sin and my dad came out of the office as Ezreal was leaving. Sin gave me a tentative smile. "Well, it's all set."

"They're coming?"

He nodded, still looking as if there was more to say but not saying it.

"When?"

"They'll be here…tonight."

"Wow." I hadn't expected them so soon. "Getting a flight on such short notice had to be awfully expensive."

Sin stuck his hands in his pockets. "My father's a conjurer. No flight required. All he needed were the coordinates for the palace. He'll work up a spell to transport them. And since the show is off for the next three weeks, the timing is perfect."

I blew out a breath. "And just like that, I'm nervous."

My father's brows lifted. "Was that Ezreal leaving? We'd better get him back. There's a lot to do. Including telling your mother. Mrs. Greenbaum—"

"Calling Her Grace right now."

"Very good." My father leaned in and kissed my cheek. "Your mom and Ezreal will handle everything. Now, I must get back to work."

"Us too," I answered. "Thanks, Dad."

"Yes," Sin said. "Thank you for the use of your phone."

"Of course. We'll get another installed so you can reach out to your folks whenever you like. In the library, maybe. Or your new apartment, since you'll want to keep in touch with your parents."

"That would be great," Sin said.

"It would be." I hadn't even thought about our new apartment lately, but then, it was a long way from being ready to move into.

"We'll add it to the punch list. See you later." My dad disappeared into his office, and Mrs. Greenbaum was already busy talking to my mom.

I gave her a little wave goodbye, then grabbed Sin's hand and led him out to the hall.

He closed the door behind us. "You're sure you're good with this?"

"Putting a phone in our apartment?"

He gave me a look. "You know what I mean. Meeting my parents."

I smiled at Sin. "I'm genuinely looking forward to it. I really am. I promise. But in the meantime, we have a date with the constable. We need to grab Birdie and get moving."

"Larsen has new information?"

"That's the message she gave to Ezreal."

"Good. Because I'd love to get this skeleton business wrapped up before my parents arrive."

"Oh?" I glanced at him as we walked toward the apartments. "Afraid your parents will think the NP is rife with crime and murder?"

He shook his head, not looking as amused as I thought he'd be. "Something like that."

That's when I realized that, despite all of my reassurances, he was still far more nervous about his parents coming to visit than I was.

The constable waited until we were all seated and the door was closed. She cleared her throat as if about to announce something of great importance. Then she opened the file in front of her. "According to his report, the ME didn't discover much more, but he was able to determine that the female victim was in her late twenties and was definitely an elf."

Birdie made a little noise of disbelief. "Then why is there no missing-person report that matches up?"

The answer hit me so hard and fast, I gasped. "Birdie. We know who she is."

Sin looked at me. "You do?"

The constable frowned. "You mean you think you know."

"Right. I can't be sure, of course, until we get some kind of DNA match, but everything in me says it's Rachel Brightmoore. George Bitterbark's ex-fiancée."

Birdie slapped the constable's desk, making her jump. "Of course!"

"Listen here," Larsen growled. "The superintendent isn't engaged."

"But he was," I said. "Long before he became superintendent. And the woman he was engaged to fits the description. Female, elf—summer not winter, but still elf—about that age, I'd imagine, and she just disappeared on him. Plus, this all happened long enough ago to work with the timeline."

Sin nodded. "You're right. It all works. Do you think George killed her?"

"That part I don't know." I wondered if I should mention Finnoula's comment about Rachel being dead to her, but decided against it. "I wouldn't think he's the murderer, but he did stop the hangar tours around that time, and we don't know why. Of course, his hiding a body in the carriage could be the answer."

The constable scribbled something in her notes. "Rachel Brightmoore, you said?"

"Yes." I pressed my hand to my forehead. "If George was really as distraught as his mother says he was, maybe it wasn't murder at all, but a terrible, terrible accident. Maybe they had an argument, and something went dreadfully wrong. That could explain a lot. Like how she seemingly disappeared and how George's mood became so dark. Can you imagine if you accidentally killed the person you'd planned to spend the rest of your life with?"

The constable looked up from what she'd been writing. "Could be. I don't know. But we're going to bring him in for questioning. Right now, however, we're about to question another suspect."

"Who?" I asked.

"LeRoy Bonfitte. I've already sent deputies to bring him in and search his premises."

"What? Why?" But I knew the answers to those questions. My head went light and my stomach queasy. I opened my mouth and took deeper breaths in an attempt to keep myself upright.

Birdie put her hand on my shoulder. "Jayne, honey, you don't look so good."

"I don't feel so good," I whispered. "It can't be LeRoy."

Larsen looked sympathetic. "I'm sorry, but what little evidence we have points to him more than George. The scrap of fabric that we know Bonfitte had access to and the stab marks consistent with scissors. It's a long shot, but if we can find the scissors that match the marks on the bones, he's as good as charged."

"That's only two pieces of evidence," I argued. "And George had motive. She broke his heart."

"We'll talk to George as well, but there's still a strong tie to Bonfitte."

I was mad now, my stomach roiling. "Two pieces of evidence is not a strong tie."

"We'll uncover more," the constable said. "We just need time."

Sin shook his head. "Please, stop your deputies. They can't bring him in."

The constable frowned. "They can and they will."

"No." Sin's sharp retort echoed through the office. "You bring him in for questioning, and he's automatically going to be guilty in some people's minds. You'll ruin his business. A business that has served this town for many years. His livelihood will suffer. Think about it. He's designing Jayne's dress. If you do this, and he's tainted by this accusation, Jayne won't be able to wear the dress. And she loves it."

I stared at Sin. I'd had no idea he understood so much. I nodded. "Sin's right. There has to be another way to do this. Not just because of my dress, but because I know in my heart that LeRoy didn't do this."

The constable shook her head. "There is no other way."

"Yes, there is." Sin looked at me for a moment, then back at the constable. The resolute set of his jaw frightened me a little. Mostly because I had a pretty good idea of what he was going to say.

"Is that so?" the constable asked. "How exactly?"

Sin's gaze was dead-on, his determination obvious. "I just need some time with the bones."

"No." The word slipped from my mouth without me even thinking about. "The cost is too high."

Birdie shook her head, looking as upset as I felt. She knew. She'd been there the last time Sin had used his gifts.

Sin turned to me. "Sweetheart, it's a sacrifice I'm willing to make."

"I appreciate that, but we're talking about bones here, not a body. How are you going to get any kind of answers from bones?"

"They'll...speak to me in their own way, I'm sure."

"That sounds to me like you aren't really certain of that. Have you worked your magic on bones before?"

"No, but—"

"Then you could be wasting your time. Literally. And you'll end up with another silver streak in your hair. Not that the silver doesn't look hot on you. It does. But how many minutes of your life would you be giving up?"

Love and tenderness were in his eyes as he looked at me. "Jayne, I love you. I know the consequences, and I accept them because it's worth it to me to use my gifts in this case to help. I don't see any other way to protect LeRoy and save your dress."

"Forget the dress. I'll get another one. Wanting to save my dress isn't a good enough reason to do this." But I knew there was another reason he wanted to do this. His parents were coming, and he wanted this case closed.

"But helping LeRoy is. So is my wanting to do this because I love you. Just let me help with this, okay? Speaking to the dead is what I do."

Birdie shrugged. "You make a mean doughnut too."

He twisted to grin at her. "Thank you."

Birdie leaned in toward us. "Let him help, Princess. It won't take long to ask those bones who did them in."

Sin nodded. "She's right. I should know instantly if I can get an answer or not. One question. A minute or two, tops."

I didn't like this at all, even though I knew it was a perfect solution. "You once told me you preferred to save the use of your skills for matters of life and death. Do you really think this qualifies?"

"For LeRoy? Yes."

I loved that he wanted to help. That he was willing. I just hated the price he had to pay. "But with time, I'm sure we could prove him innocent. You'd really be doing this to expedite things."

He nodded slowly. "I'm okay with that. In this instance, it's worth losing a minute or two of my life to put all of this behind us."

"If that's all you lose." I could feel tears welling up. It was all this stupid stress of the wedding and his parents suddenly on their way and then Sin being so wonderfully sweet and caring. I sniffed and gave a little nod. I couldn't stand in his way. Not when he had a stake in this as well. "Please, no longer than a minute or two of contact."

"I promise." He turned to the constable, who looked like we'd all been talking in Greek. "I suppose I need some kind of official permission granted to have access to the bones?"

Her eyes narrowed. "You're saying you can talk to those bones? And find out who the murderer is?"

"I am a necromancer, as I know you know. That's what we do. We speak to the dead. And allow them to speak for themselves."

That wasn't all a necromancer could do. But there was no point in Sin expanding on the full extent of his gifts. He'd only end up scaring the constable.

She tapped the end of her pencil on the desktop for an agonizingly long time before answering, "All right. But I want to be there. If this is going to be official, it's got to be properly documented."

"Naturally." He put his hands on the arm of the

chair like he was about to get up, then stopped. "Can we go now? We really need to get this taken care of."

"Certainly."

"Great." He stood. "Just please, call off your deputies until I talk to the remains. LeRoy won't go anywhere. He'll still be there if they tell us he's the killer."

Larsen frowned, then nodded. "All right. But if you don't find out something that says he's not involved, we're bringing him in immediately."

Sin nodded. "Understood."

She picked up the radio handset on her desk, squeezed the button, and spoke. "Deputy Verne, come in."

The radio squawked with his reply. "This is Deputy Verne."

"Stand down on Bonfitte and return to the station."

After a moment of silence, he answered, "Copy that. Returning to station."

She placed the handset back on her desk, then stood up, adjusting her utility belt. "This had better get us some answers. Actionable answers. Because you realize I can't rightly arrest someone just because you say the bones whispered clues to you. I need something that leads to hard evidence. Understand?"

Sin got to his feet. "Completely. But what the bones tell us might also keep you from arresting the wrong person."

He let Larsen go out first, then Birdie, but as I passed him, he put his hand on my arm to stop me. "I may not be able to give the constable what she wants. Even if the bones reveal the murderer, that doesn't mean they'll point me to evidence Larsen can use for an arrest."

"I was thinking that too." I tucked a strand of hair behind my ear. "As long as you can find out for sure who the murderer is…we'll figure out how to bring them to justice afterward."

"That doesn't sound exactly legal."

"Yeah, I'm aware. But desperate times—"

"Call for desperate measures. Whatever we have to do, we're doing it together."

I smiled. Then took his hand. He was so the guy for me.

We walked out of the station that way, hand in hand. And the overwhelming weight that had been resting on me felt diminished just by having Sinclair at my side.

We followed Larsen's police crawler to the ME's office, which was attached to the morgue. It wasn't a place I'd ever been before, but I had been to the one in Nocturne Falls. It was in the hospital basement, which seemed fitting.

The North Pole morgue was just a big gray building.

We parked outside and met Larsen at the door.

"Is Dr. Charming here?"

"No." She unhooked a ring of keys from her utility belt. "I didn't think there was any reason to pull him from his patients."

"I suppose not." I moved a little closer to Sin. Morgues didn't exactly creep me out, but visiting one wasn't exactly my idea of happy fun time either.

Birdie didn't seem phased by it.

Larsen unlocked the door, went inside, and flipped some switches. Lights and soft, oddly cheerful instrumental music came on.

The decent-sized foyer held one narrow leather couch and four matching chairs, along with a small table. A spray of magazines, all outdated, sat on the table. I couldn't help but wonder who might use a waiting room like this.

The antiseptic smell wasn't unpleasant, but it wasn't something I wanted to dab behind my ears either.

Birdie's nose wrinkled. Apparently, she wasn't fond of the smell, but then, werewolves had a much more sensitive olfactory system than elves did.

On either side of the foyer were doors. One was marked Office. One wasn't marked at all.

Larsen headed for the unmarked one. "This way."

Birdie looked at me and shrugged as if to say, *I hope this works*.

I hoped it worked too. There was a lot riding on this. Namely, LeRoy's reputation and livelihood. And our shot at capturing the killer, who might still walk free in the North Pole.

We followed Larsen through the door, then through another small room that held a few filing cabinets, then into the larger room I'd been anticipating.

The antiseptic smell was stronger in here. The room held two stainless-steel tables. I was pretty sure they were used for autopsies, but I wasn't going to dwell on that.

The far wall was what concerned us. The three rows of rectangular drawers, also stainless steel, held my attention with as much pull as a flashing neon sign. I couldn't look away from them. What drawer was the skeleton in?

Sinclair nudged me.

I tore my gaze from the morgue wall to look at him. He pointed, and I followed his gesture.

Larsen was taking a large black bag from a horizontal filing cabinet against the opposite wall. "These are the remains."

Sin leaned in. "Bones aren't refrigerated," he said to me.

"Oh, right." I felt a little dumb. But that was okay. It was still better than being freaked out by where I was.

Larsen put the bag on one of the stainless-steel tables and unzipped it.

The tiniest bit of smooth bone was visible. Creamy white and visibly porous. Much easier to look at than a body, I had to say. My nerves settled.

Sin rolled his shoulders and approached the bag.

I pulled out my phone and opened up the timer app. "No more than two minutes."

He glanced at me, a little amusement in his eyes. "It may take longer than that to make the connection."

"Sin." That wasn't what he'd promised me.

"Sweetheart, if I'm going to do this, I'm not going to cut things short just because it takes longer than a hundred and twenty seconds."

"Thank you," Larsen said. She was at the far end of the table.

Birdie linked her arm through mine. "It'll be okay. Sinclair's got a long, long life ahead of him. A minute or two isn't going to matter a wink."

I knew there was no point in arguing. My mouth firmed into a hard line, and I sighed. I put my phone away. That was as close as I was going to get to acquiescing.

With a quick, reassuring smile in my direction, Sin pushed his sleeves back and stood over the bag, hands above the opening, fingers wide. "Bear in mind, I've never done this with bones. I don't know what to expect, but I'll do everything I can to get answers."

We all nodded.

He took a breath. "Here goes."

I tensed as Sinclair reached into the bag and made contact with the bones.

I'd seen Sin use his gifts to bring the dead temporarily back to life again in Nocturne Falls, so I knew what to expect.

There was still something a little unsettling about the act. And something a little awe-inducing about the fact that I was marrying a man who could do this.

He stiffened as if the breath caught in his lungs. His eyes went silver white. No pupils, no irises, just all glowing silver-white light. His lips parted, but no sound came out for a few seconds.

Finally, he spoke, his voice thin and far away, but then, it wasn't directed at us. "Who are you?"

In the silence that followed, the tick of the wall clock echoed like a sledgehammer whacking concrete.

He nodded like he was listening, then he spoke to us in a stronger voice. "It's her. Rachel Brightmoore."

"I knew it," I whispered.

Birdie squeezed my arm against her like the thrill of it all was getting to her. "Ask her who killed her."

Sin nodded. "How did you die, Rachel?"

His glowing gaze was focused off into the distance, but I wondered what he was actually seeing. Blackness? Or visions that Rachel was sharing with him? Or was he just hearing her voice in his head? This was so different than the time he'd brought Myra Grimshaw back to life in Nocturne Falls. We'd been able to talk to her. But then, she hadn't been dead for as long as Rachel had.

He grimaced and made sounds of discomfort, then what could only be described as a moan of pain.

I lurched forward, but Birdie held on to me.

His face relaxed, and he spoke again. "Thank you for sharing that with me."

With a shudder, he let go of the bones. He planted his hands on the table and leaned on them heavily. He took deep breaths, his head tilted down like he was looking into the bag. His eyes were back to normal, but he seemed shaken.

"Sin, are you okay?" I glanced at my phone. I

hadn't turned the timer off. Five minutes, twenty-six seconds. Snowballs.

He nodded, but didn't answer, which told me he wasn't okay.

I went to his side, putting my arm around him. "You need sugar, don't you?"

He nodded again, still breathing in deep gulps.

"We're going to get you some right away." I looked at Larsen. "Is there anything here? A vending machine? An employee lounge with snacks?"

"No, sorry."

"You have doughnuts at the station?"

She nodded. "There's all kinds of pastries and sweets in the breakroom. We'll find something."

"Then let's go."

Birdie and I helped Sin into the crawler, where he lay down across the back seats. I drove, following Larsen, who didn't spare the gas. That made me happy.

While we were on the way, Birdie dug a hard toffee out of her purse. "Here, Sinclair. It's not much, but it might help a little."

"Thanks." He took it, and the crinkle of the wrapper being discarded followed.

"You okay back there?" I asked.

"I will be. The toffee is helping."

"Good. Anything you want to tell us now before we get to the station?"

"Nothing that can't be shared."

"All right, rest then."

He did, and when we got to the station, he had no issues walking in on his own power. He was still obviously lagging, but with some more sugar, he'd be back to normal in no time.

Larsen was more than accommodating on the sugar front, getting us settled in her office, then slipping out only to return with a can of cherry cola and two paper plates piled high with goodies. Cookies, muffins, cupcakes, brownies, blondies, and a few packaged snack cakes.

She set the haul on the desk in front of Sin. "Quite a few of the spouses like to bake and send things in, so we always have a lot to choose from. And there's plenty more, so don't be shy."

"Thank you." He popped the top on the soda and took a long drink. He set the can down and picked up a brownie. After he took a big bite of that, I could see a little color coming back into his face.

That gave me great relief.

Larsen folded her hands on the desk. "Better?"

He nodded. "Much."

"When you're ready, then, what did you learn?"

He took another bite of the brownie, and once he'd swallowed that, he began. "First of all, her answers came to me in snippets of memories. Like watching little pieces of a movie. There was no recollection of being stabbed. No recollection of being murdered, actually. What she showed me was her having tea with two people I can only assume were George and his mother. Looked like in George's house. Or maybe it was the mother's. They were discussing the wedding, then Rachel started to feel poorly." He paused. "I could feel her distress like it was my own."

He drank a little soda before continuing. "She lay down to rest in a guest room, and when she woke up, still sick, she was in a small dark room that was bitterly cold." He paused, and a terrible light shone in his eyes. "She screamed for help until her voice was gone. Eventually, she had nothing left. No energy. No ability to go on. Her body was racked with chills as the sickness got worse. She went to sleep and didn't wake up again."

Birdie sucked in a breath and put her hand to her mouth. "That poor child. It sounds like she might have been poisoned. And left to die."

We were all quiet for a long moment after that.

Larsen, who was, I suppose, more used to this kind of thing than the rest of us, spoke first. "I'll ask Dr. Charming to do a toxicology report, although having only bones to work with might make that more difficult."

"That would be good," I said, still distressed by what Sin had learned.

Larsen went on. "And now we can confirm she

didn't die in the carriage. That fits with what we found. Or rather, didn't find since there was a distinct lack of evidence at the scene. I'd guess her body remained where she was for long enough to decompose, and then the bones were recently moved."

"But why move them at all?" I shook my head. "Putting them in the Crystal Carriage seems like a very deliberate act. So what was the point of it? To derail our wedding? To frame LeRoy? If it's the latter, why wait all these years? There's more to this than we know."

"Agreed," Larsen said. "We only have part of the picture."

I nodded. "And we won't have the whole thing until we know who's responsible. At least we know her memories don't include being stabbed."

The constable nodded. "That must have happened post-mortem."

I crossed my arms. "Again, done to frame LeRoy."

Larsen flicked her gaze at me. "We don't know that was the reason."

My brows shot up. "Someone stabbed her with scissors, then left a scrap of fabric under her remains that matches a dress made by LeRoy, and you don't think that looks like a frame job?"

She frowned. "I understand that you have a bias toward him, but we can't rule out anyone at this point. Maybe it was done to frame him, or maybe he had a motive we don't know about."

"Then let's find out." I got up. "I'm going to talk to him. I'm going to ask him about Rachel and see what he says."

Larsen stood too. "I'm going with you. With all due respect, an officer of the law needs to be there."

"I completely understand." I didn't wait for her. I just left, Sin and Birdie following behind me. I was mad. I *did* understand that Larsen was doing her job, but I really couldn't see how LeRoy was involved in this.

I called him on the drive over. He picked up right away. I spoke as soon as the line went live. "LeRoy? It's Jayne."

"Princess, how lovely to hear from you. To what do I owe the pleasure?"

"I'm on my way over with Constable Larsen. We need to talk to you about an ongoing case. I just wanted to give you a heads-up."

"I see. Well, I appreciate that, and I'm happy to help."

"I want you to know that I'm on your side. I hope my faith in you is well placed."

A moment of silence followed. Then he cleared his throat. "Am I in some sort of trouble?"

I knew I shouldn't say too much, or I could be putting myself in hot water as well. Royal immunity went only so far. "I hope not. We'll be there in a few minutes. Don't panic. Just prepare yourself to answer some questions."

"I will. Thank you."

"Don't thank me yet." I hung up.

Sin was giving me a look. I could feel it. "What?"

"You're putting yourself in a precarious position."

"I agree," Birdie said. "If he's guilty, you've just aided and abetted him."

I glanced at her through the rearview mirror. "I didn't give him any details. I didn't even mention Rachel's name."

She pursed her lips. "That's the only saving grace."

Sin shook his head. "I know you're upset, sweetheart. But we have to do this the right way."

"Sure, to a point. Larsen seems like she has it out for LeRoy. Someone needs to be on his side."

I found a parking space near the shop, and we went in.

LeRoy met us at the entrance. His brow was furrowed and his posture rigid with tension. He bowed stiffly. "Princess Jayne."

I took his hands and squeezed them. "It's all going to be all right."

Larsen came in right behind us.

I dropped LeRoy's hands and made the introductions. "LeRoy, this is Constable Larsen. Constable, this is the royal couturier, LeRoy Bonfitte."

Instantly, LeRoy shed all traces of anxiety and was his usual charming self. With a gracious smile, he extended his hand. "Constable, it's my pleasure to meet you. What a wonderful job you do of keeping our town so peaceful and safe."

She shook his hand, but didn't react much more than that. She was hard to read in that moment. She certainly didn't seem impressed with anything. Not the shop, not LeRoy's title, not his welcoming attitude. "Is there somewhere we can talk?"

He spread his arms. "My shop is my home. We can speak anywhere you like. But perhaps we'd be more comfortable in the grand salon? There are plenty of spots to sit there." He turned and softly called out, "Charlotte?"

His assistant appeared from the back. "Sir?"

"Please watch the shop. I'll be in the grand salon for a bit and don't want to be disturbed."

"Yes, sir."

We followed LeRoy back to the very place where I'd recently stood in the dress of my dreams. The four of us settled onto the couches. The constable stayed on her feet.

Then she started in. "Do you recall a woman by the name of Rachel Brightmoore?"

LeRoy's gaze narrowed in recollection. "Brightmoore...just a moment. Was she a summer elf?"

The constable nodded.

LeRoy shook his head. "That was ages ago." He glanced at me. "About the time of your christening, I'd say. Or before it. Or right after." He returned his attention to the constable. "I'd have to check my files to be certain."

"That would be good," Larsen said. "What was your relationship with her?"

"Relationship?" LeRoy looked amused. "The same as it is with every woman who walks through those doors. To dress her to the best of my ability. I was designing a gown for her. A wedding gown, if memory serves."

Larsen's stony expression remained unchanged. "You're a very popular designer, aren't you?"

"Thanks to the patronage of the royal family, that's true."

"And you have been for some time, correct?"

"Yes. Well over sixty years."

"If I wanted you to design a dress for me, what would the process be like?"

LeRoy didn't hesitate. "I'd start by checking my appointment book to see what my next available opening is. Typically, I'm booked quite a few months out, and that's for regular customers. For a new client, it can take a substantial while longer to get them in. In fact, there's a waiting list for new clients."

"And it's been like that for a while?"

"Yes. It's just how my business works."

Larsen paced a few steps to the right, bringing her closer to LeRoy. "How did Miss Brightmoore, who wasn't even a citizen of the realm, happen to get an appointment with you, then?"

He put a hand to his chin, gaze narrowing in thought. "I'm trying to remember the circumstances."

While LeRoy thought, Larsen turned and went left, hands behind her back like she had all day to wear a path in the shop's pale blue carpeting.

Suddenly, his finger went up. "It's coming back to me. Another patron gave up her standing appointment so that Miss Brightmoore could come in."

Larsen stopped pacing. "Another patron? Who?"

LeRoy smiled, clearly pleased that he'd pulled the information from the recesses of his memory. "Mrs. Finnoula Bitterbark."

Birdie and I looked at each other. Her brows were raised. And I understood. Finnoula had cared enough to make sure Rachel had a dress from LeRoy. If she'd gotten an inkling that Rachel was going to break off the engagement, Finnoula could have been upset enough to do something drastic about it.

And Finnoula had only been in the beginning stages of her illness when this had all happened. She would have still had the strength to say, move a body.

Even so, I shrugged. Mostly because I was still leaning toward George at this point. "It could mean Finnoula's involved. Unless you think she was in on it with LeRoy. Which I don't. It probably just means she was trying to help out her future daughter-in-law."

Birdie nodded. "I agree. I think we should go see her again."

The constable turned toward Birdie. "You went to see her? About this case?"

"No," I chimed in quickly. Birdie didn't need to take this one on. She'd only been along for the ride at Finnoula's. "We were trying to find out why her son put an end to the hangar tours."

The constable's unconvinced smirk was so brief I almost didn't catch it. "And did you?"

I sighed. "No. In fact, I haven't even spoken to George yet. I wanted to ask him to restart the tours in honor of our wedding."

Sin smiled. "That would be nice. My parents would enjoy that, I think. My dad's always been a car guy. And I realize there aren't really any cars in there, but the vehicles would interest him all the same."

I leaned in toward Sin. "You know I can get him in there regardless of whether the tours are happening or not."

Larsen cleared her throat. "If we could get back to the subject at hand—"

"Which one?" I asked. "Finnoula? George? Rachel? How about we do whatever we need to do to clear LeRoy's name?"

Larsen snapped, "I can't do that until the real murderer is found."

LeRoy recoiled. "Murderer? Is that what happened to Rachel? Why she disappeared?"

I nodded. "I'm afraid so. How far did you get with her dress?"

Lines bracketed his mouth, giving a glimpse into his age. "I only had a muslin done, so it wasn't much of a loss, but it still pains me to hear that such a sweet girl met such a terrible end."

On a hunch, I asked a new question. "Had she picked out her fabric?"

"Yes." He narrowed his eyes again, thinking. "I'm sure I can find a sample of it." He stood, but didn't go anywhere. "Would you like me to get it?"

"Yes." The four of us responded in unison.

"It'll just take me a moment." He left.

I started checking things off on my fingers. "We need to talk to Finnoula. Then we need to speak to George about the tours, which I can do by myself since I also want to bring up restarting the tours." I turned to Sin. "If there's anything that would make your parents stay here more comfortable, then we should let Ezreal know immediately."

"They're not high-maintenance people. Although my mother's diet has some peculiarities—"

"Brains?" Birdie whispered.

He laughed softly. "No, she's gluten-free."

"Oh." Birdie shrugged. "Just wondering."

LeRoy came back with a garment bag slung over his arm. "I couldn't find a small sample, but I've made a few dresses from the fabric, so I brought one of those. It's not the most traditional bridal fabric, but as I recall that was what Rachel liked about it. I remember that of all the swatches I showed her, this was the one she fell in love with instantly."

A question popped into my head. "Would you have given her a sample of the fabric?"

"Absolutely."

I looked at Larsen. "If Rachel had a sample, George could have gotten his hands on it."

She nodded. "Possible." She glanced at LeRoy. "The dress?"

He laid the garment bag over one of the chairs, then unzipped it, revealing the dress. "This is a retired design from my archives, but it's the same fabric Rachel chose."

The dress was ivory shot through with pearl and silver threads. An exact match for the snippet of fabric Birdie had found in the carriage.

"Son of a nutcracker." This was not good. This felt like one more piece of evidence against LeRoy. Like whoever had wanted to frame him had known just how to do it.

Larsen put her hands on her hips. "You're positive that's the fabric Rachel picked out?"

LeRoy nodded with some hesitation. "Yes. Is there a problem?"

"Just that it matches a scrap found with the remains." Her shoulders went back a little. "This doesn't help your case."

He shook his head, fear in his eyes. "Why would I do anything to hurt that girl? She was my client. And about to marry into the Bitterbark family. There's no logical reason for me to do anything to stop that."

Larsen's eyes narrowed. "I agree. Which is the main reason I'm not taking you in. Lack of motive. But you're not to leave the NP, you understand?"

I exhaled in relief.

The fear left his gaze, and he lifted his chin in what could only be described as defiance. "Of course I understand. I wouldn't leave anyway. I have far too much work to do on Princess Jayne's wedding gown."

I smiled at his not-so-subtle reminder to the constable. I stood. "We'll leave you to it, then, LeRoy. Thank you for your time. I know how valuable it is."

He bowed slightly. "For you, Your Highness, anything." He cast a sideways glance at the constable, then gathered the garment bag and stalked off.

I knew he was still a suspect, but I had to snicker to myself. LeRoy was a character, and I loved it. "All right, we should get going. Too much to do and too little time to do it in."

"Agreed," Larsen said. "I'll call Finnoula Bitterbark and set up a time to interview her."

"About that," I started. "She might not see you."

"I'm the law. She doesn't have a choice."

"Be that as it may, she's not a well woman. We only got in to see her because my uncle's secretary, Mamie, was with us, and Mamie is an old friend of hers."

"What are you proposing?"

Nothing actually, but since Larsen had opened the door, I was walking through. "How about Birdie and I go see her again, with Mamie if need be? Then we'll fill you in. That would free you up to follow whatever other leads you have."

Larsen seemed to ponder that for a moment. "That wouldn't be official, though."

"It would be if you deputized Birdie. You had mentioned doing that when we first discovered the bones. You know with her experience, she'd be sure we get all the right questions answered."

The constable nodded. "I suppose that would be all right. If Miss Caruthers is agreeable."

Birdie stood up. "Certainly."

Larsen nodded at her. "Then I hereby deputize you in the name of the North Pole Department of Law. You're authorized to conduct interviews in the Rachel Brightmoore case." She put her hands on her hips. "And I expect to hear back from you as soon as your conversation with Finnoula is done."

"You got it," Birdie said.

"Absolutely," I promised. "May I ask what you'll be working on?"

"I'm going to see George about why the tours

were stopped and find out more about the dissolution of his engagement."

"Great. Then I guess we'll both have information to share."

Sin, Birdie, and I didn't waste another second, immediately getting back into the crawler and heading to the factory.

I called Mamie on the way.

"Santa's office, Mamie speaking."

"Mamie, it's Jayne. We need to speak to Finnoula again. Do you think she'll be more responsive if you're along, or do you think our tea with her was enough of an introduction that she'll be friendly?"

"I think she'll be friendly. I genuinely believe she enjoyed our visit. And you're the princess. She's not going to refuse to see you."

"I realize that, but I want it to be on good terms."

"You'll be fine without me. May I ask why you're going to speak to her again? New developments?"

I turned toward the Bitterbark's since picking up Mamie was no longer necessary. "Yes. Finnoula made it possible for Rachel to see LeRoy about having a wedding dress made. He got as far as sewing a muslin sample for her to try. And she had fabric picked out. Fabric that matches a scrap found under her bones in the carriage."

Mamie made an unhappy sound. "That's not good for LeRoy, is it?"

"No. Not at all."

"Let me know if there's anything else I can do to help. I like LeRoy, and I don't believe for a moment that he's capable of murder. You know, he made my second and fourth wedding dresses? He's such a talented man and just a lovely person."

"I agree. I'll keep you posted. Thanks." I hung up as we approached the Bitterbarks' townhouse.

I parked, and the three of us got out.

Sin stayed by the crawler. "Are you sure you want me to go with you? She might not welcome a strange man into her home."

"You're not exactly a strange man. You're about to become the Prince Consort. It'll be fine."

"Come on," Birdie said. "Besides, you saw Rachel's visions. I'd be interested to know if what she showed you took place in this house. You won't know unless you see it in person. Might give you some new insight into her murder too."

"Good point. I'm coming." He walked with us to the door.

I knocked and we waited.

Elma answered again. She dipped into a curtsy. "Princess Jayne. What a nice surprise."

I wasn't sure I believed that since her thin smile didn't reach her eyes, but I also realized our visits made extra work for her. "Hello, Elma. Birdie, Consort Sinclair, and I would like to speak to Finnoula for a few moments. Official business this time."

She nodded. "Certainly. I'll let her know. She's having lunch with George." She opened the door wider. "Please come in."

"George is here?" I wasn't expecting that, although I guessed it was later in the day than I realized.

We entered, and she shut the door. "Yes, lunch is a little early today because he's got meetings this afternoon. He never misses a lunch with his mother."

Was she trying to guilt me into leaving? I smiled with all the royal authority I could muster. "As much as I hate to intrude on their meal, I have questions for him as well." I wasn't backing down. I wasn't coming back at a later time. Too much was at stake.

She *almost* frowned at me. "I'll let them know."

"Very good."

She took off into another part of the house.

Birdie leaned in. "Are you sure we should be interrupting?"

"Yes. We need answers. And we're getting them today."

Sin chuckled softly. "That's my girl."

Elma returned shortly. "If you'll please follow me."

She took us through the house and into the dining room. The entire house, while slightly dated, was warm and welcoming. It felt lived in, but in the best possible way. A family had been raised here.

But then again, Rachel's life had probably ended here.

It was a sobering thought and one that steeled me for what lay ahead.

Elma preceded us into the dining room. "Princess Jayne, Consort Sinclair, and Ms. Caruthers."

"Please," I said as we entered. "Don't get up."

Finnoula remained seated, but George was already out of his chair. He bowed. "Your Graces. This is an unexpected honor. To what do we owe the pleasure of your visit?"

My smile was a little grim, but there was no helping that. Our visit wasn't social. "We have some questions that need answers. May we sit? I promise we won't take more of your time than necessary."

"Yes, of course." He started pulling chairs out. He'd been a handsome man once upon a time, but the stresses of his life and his losses had worn him down into something far more ordinary.

My heart went out to him. A man so dedicated to his mother didn't seem like the type to take the life of the woman he loved, even if she had broken his heart. "Thank you."

We all sat at the end of the table, myself in the middle, Birdie and Sin flanking me.

Finnoula smiled hesitantly. "It's nice to see you again, whatever reason brings you here."

"Thank you. Like I said, we need some

questions answered. And while I'm very sorry to interrupt your lunch, it's an urgent matter."

George wiped his mouth with a cloth napkin, then turned to look at us. "I hope we can give you answers."

"I'm sure you can. One of the things I need to know is why you canceled the Hangar Nine tours all those years ago."

He shifted his eyes back to his plate, and several uncomfortable moments went by before he spoke again. "I'm ashamed to say it was for personal reasons. I proposed to a woman in front of the Crystal Carriage. It's a very romantic object. But I'm sure I don't have to explain that to you. Anyway, when that engagement fell apart..." He shrugged, and a weak smile bent his mouth. "Not a great excuse, I suppose. But I was hurt. And angry. I hope you can understand."

"I do. Love and heartache make us do... questionable things."

He nodded, staring at his plate again. The muscles in his jaw twitched, and the sadness in his eyes was replaced with a cold light. His hand tightened on the cloth napkin until his knuckles went white. "They certainly do."

The little hairs on the back of my neck stood up. Could he be guilty? I'd briefly thought so before, but now? It was starting to seem like a serious possibility. In fact, in this moment, he seemed very capable of murder.

Then he took a breath and exhaled, and the sudden, sharp darkness surrounding him went with it. He was back to being sad-eyed George.

"What other questions do you have, Princess?" Finnoula quickly turned the conversation away from her son.

I did have questions for her, but it was nearly impossible to stop watching George. I took one last look at him before starting to answer her, but she spoke again.

"Elma, the tea's gone cold. Could you fix a fresh pot?"

"Yes, ma'am." Elma left, albeit a little reluctantly. I was sure our conversation was interesting. Especially since Finnoula had told us during our earlier visit that the subject of Rachel was basically off-limits.

Finnoula's smile grew a little. "I thought perhaps privacy would be better."

I nodded. "Perhaps it would be. But I have one more question for George." I looked at him again. "Can you tell me why Rachel broke up with you?"

His gaze turned distant, and his shoulders slumped. "I don't know. That's part of what made it so hard, I guess. She just disappeared from my life. From our house, actually. She'd been staying here. Then one morning, we woke up to find her gone."

Beside me, Birdie practically bristled. His story certainly matched what Sin had seen.

George took a breath that seemed as labored as his mother's. "I reached out to her in every way I knew how, but all my attempts at communication were met with silence. After a little while, I took the hint and gave up."

Finnoula grunted in obvious disgust. "She could have at least had the decency to return the ring."

If George had killed Rachel, he was covering it well. The story about her just disappearing could be a great smoke screen. And so close to the truth of what Rachel had shared with Sin. But if George hadn't killed her, then that would explain why he had no idea what had really happened.

Not quite ready to reveal everything just yet, I turned to Finnoula. "What can you tell me about Rachel's relationship with LeRoy Bonfitte? You gave up your own appointment with him so that she could have a wedding dress made, didn't you?"

"I did. And I was happy to do it. Rachel was..." She glanced at George.

He shrugged. "There's no point in not telling them."

Sympathy filled her eyes. "But, George—"

"I'm fine, Mother." He stiffened a little. Was he bracing himself against the memories? Or was it his anger returning? "Tell them what they want to know."

With a sigh, Finnoula took a deep, difficult inhale and went on. "Rachel was a beautiful soul, inside and out. That's why her sudden coldness came as such a shock. Why it hurt so much. But back to the dress. Why wouldn't I give up my appointment for her? I wasn't losing a son. I was gaining a daughter."

Would Sin's mom think that about me?

A soft smile played on Finnoula's mouth. "She really wanted to have her dress made here, as a remembrance of the North Pole, and to honor George's heritage. I thought that was sweet."

"As a remembrance?" That was an odd word choice.

Finnoula nodded. "They were getting married in California. She was starting a job there as a pharmaceutical sales rep." She touched the handle of her teacup, but didn't pick it up. "I was going to move there with them. With my husband passed and my other children already in the mortal world, if George wasn't going to be here, what reason did I have to stay? And warm weather is supposed to be good for my illness."

I nodded. "Sinclair told me about that. Was it your idea to move with them, then?"

"No." She shook her head. "It was Rachel's. To be honest, I would never have imposed on a newlywed couple." Her smile faltered. "My other children never offered. But Rachel genuinely seemed like she wanted me to move with them."

"She did," George said quietly. "She was like that. Warm. Generous. Kindhearted."

"Then I can understand why it was such a blow when things didn't go as planned."

He nodded.

I couldn't put it off any longer. I had to tell them what we'd discovered. "There's more to why we came than just these questions, as you might have imagined. We've come with information about Rachel."

That took the smile off Finnoula's face, and

George looked at me with such expectation that I knew immediately he was going to take my news harder than I'd realized.

He swallowed in what seemed like an attempt to calm himself. "Is she back? Is she here in town?"

"In a manner of speaking." My heart hurt, but the words had to be spoken. I watched George's face carefully for any telling reaction as I revealed the truth about Rachel. "I'm very sorry, but we've found her remains."

"Her…" George went pale. He put his trembling hands flat on the table, maybe in an effort to calm them. "You mean she's deceased."

"Yes."

With some effort, Finnoula got up and wheeled her oxygen tank around to George. She put her arm around him, bent her head, and whispered something I couldn't make out.

Quietly, I continued, hoping, I think, to give them some peace. "She has actually been deceased for a very long while. In fact, I'd say that's the reason she disappeared on you." I glanced at Sinclair, looking for confirmation that it was all right to tell them what he'd seen.

He nodded, then opened his mouth as if to speak.

"Go on," I said softly.

"I'm very sorry for your loss." He cleared his throat, hesitating. "As you probably know, I'm a necromancer."

Finnoula looked up. "Yes, I remember the hullabaloo. I'm sorry a small minority made so much noise about that."

"Thank you."

Her eyes went wide with sudden realization. "Did you…use your skills on Rachel?"

He took a breath. "I did."

She sagged into the chair next to George and took her son's hand. Both of them stared at Sin like he was about to reveal the meaning of life to them.

George swallowed audibly. "What did you find out?"

"She was murdered." Sin's head bent with the weight of the words. "I don't think I can say more than that due to the investigation."

Birdie shook her head. "No, you shouldn't."

I knew what she and Sin must be thinking, because I was thinking it too. We were in the same room with the last two people who'd seen Rachel alive. The last two people she'd shared a meal with. The same meal where she might have ingested poison.

The doorbell chimed, echoing through the house.

George let go of his mother's hand and pushed to his feet. "I'll get it."

"Let Elma get it," she said. "It's not important right now."

Pounding on the door followed.

George frowned. "That doesn't sound like it's not important. I guess Elma's busy with your tea." He looked at us. "If you'll excuse me."

"Of course," I said.

A loud bang came next, then a sharp crack. It sounded to me very much like the front door had been breached.

"George and Finnoula Bitterbark, this is Constable Larsen. Make yourself known."

George went out into the hall. "What's all this about, Constable?"

"We have a warrant to search this house."

Finnoula gasped. I got to my feet, as did Birdie and Sinclair. Birdie and I rushed to the hall while Sinclair gave Finnoula his arm to lean on and helped her out. Elma was already in the hall when we got there. She quickly came to Finnoula's other side and hooked her arm around Finnoula's waist.

Finnoula might have been frail in body, but her mind and her spirit were strong. She stared Larsen down. "What's the meaning of all this, Constable? Why do you want to search this house?"

Constable Larsen straightened. "We received an anonymous tip that Rachel Brightmoore was murdered in this house."

Finnoula's mouth opened, but no sound came out. Then she fainted dead away. As petite as she was, she slipped out of Elma's and Sin's grasp, crumpling to the floor.

Elma knelt at Finnoula's side and gently took hold of her shoulders. "Mrs. Bitterbark. *Mrs. Bitterbark.*"

Anger and concern flashing in his eyes, George stepped between his mother and Constable Larsen. "Go. Search. Do whatever you need. Just leave my mother alone. She's not a well woman."

"My apologies. Upsetting her was not my intent." Larsen gestured to the deputies behind her. "Let's go."

As they dispersed, Finnoula came to with a thin, wheezing breath. Her eyes were wild and round, searching for something. She reached out, grabbing hold of the front of Elma's uniform. "George. George. I need George."

He was on his knees beside her in an instant. "I'm right here, Mama."

Finnoula seemed to calm at the sound of his voice. One hand reached for him, the other clenched tighter on the front of Elma's uniform, pulling it open.

A chain around Elma's neck swung free.

On it dangled a ring with a big fiery-yellow center stone surrounded by sparkling diamonds.

George's head turned like it was on a swivel. His eyes widened. In a split-second move, he snatched the ring and pulled his mother out of Elma's grasp. Fire lit his eyes, and his entire body shook with new energy.

Elma was caught by the chain. She tried to back up, but couldn't go more than a few inches. "Let me go."

But George held fast. His voice came out ragged with emotion. "Not until you tell me why you have Rachel's engagement ring around your neck."

Elma reared back, snapping the chain. "That should have been my ring. You should have married me."

"You're insane," Finnoula whispered. George helped her to stand.

Elma pushed to her feet. "Don't try me, old woman." Her eyes darted toward the front door.

"Sin," I whispered. "Don't let her get away."

Elma glared at me, growling out a single word. *"You."*

I jerked back. "What did I do?"

Sin grabbed hold of her. She tried to pull out of his grasp, but he was too strong. "You don't deserve happiness. No one does."

Birdie shook her head. "She's nutty. I'm getting Larsen." She headed off down the hall.

I looked at George. "Are you certain that's Rachel's ring?"

He opened his hand and glanced at the ring, then nodded. "Yes. I can see the words I engraved on the inside of the band."

Elma twisted in Sin's grip, trying to break free. "Let me go."

"You're not going anywhere," he said. "Except to a holding cell."

Birdie and Larsen joined us. Larsen had her radio in her hand and was speaking to someone. "Roger that. Thanks." She pinched the handset again. "Givens, Thurmon, return to the hall."

Larsen looked at George. "You can confirm that's the engagement ring you gave to Miss Brightmoore?"

"Yes. Like I just told Her Highness, I had it engraved. This is definitely the ring I bought Rachel."

"Very good. Thank you," Larsen said. "One of my deputies at the station was tracing the anonymous call we got. It came from this house." She shook her head as she approached Elma. "I guess you thought you could frame George, huh? Or maybe Mrs. Bitterbark? Not a great play bringing us to you, but then again, most criminals are pretty dumb."

Elma vibrated with anger. "George is the dumb one. For falling in love with that summer elf."

Larsen gave Elma a look. "So you think keeping that engagement ring on a chain around your neck was a smart move?" She snorted. "Criminals."

I almost laughed. The constable didn't exactly

have a long history of dealing with these kinds of offenders, but who was I to remind her of that at a time like this?

Larsen pulled cuffs off her belt and, with Sin's assistance, got them on Elma. "We'll take her down to the station for questioning, and we'll be keeping her in a cell there until trial." She looked at George. "I'm sorry, but we're going to need the ring for evidence, at least for a little while."

Finnoula patted her son's arm even as she held on to it. "It's all right."

He nodded. "I understand." He took one last long look at it, then handed it over to Larsen.

The deputies arrived from wherever they'd been searching in the house.

Larsen took Elma by the elbow and moved her forward toward the older deputy, Givens. "Get her into the crawler."

"Yes, ma'am." He led Elma out, the other deputy following along.

Larsen faced us. "We'll question her thoroughly. Hopefully, we'll get a complete confession. Even if we don't, the ring is pretty strong evidence."

Finnoula kept a firm grip on her son. "Do you really think she killed Rachel?"

Larsen's mouth firmed into a tight line. "The ME found winter primrose toxin in Rachel's bones. Would your housekeeper have access to such a thing?"

George and Finnoula both looked perplexed.

Then Sin spoke up. "Winter primrose flowers are dried and ground up as an additive to reindeer feed. It helps the reindeer fly, but the flowers are toxic to elves in large quantities. That's why the stable workers always wear gloves when they feed the reindeer." He lifted one shoulder. "I learned that in class recently."

I thought about what he'd said. "Rachel was a summer elf. I'm guessing the effect on her would have been a lot greater. Probably wouldn't have taken such large amounts either."

Finnoula put her hand to her mouth. "Elma's father works at the stables. He has for years. I think he's a farrier."

"That gives Elma access to the toxin," Larsen said.

It was starting to come together now. "She must have slipped it into something Rachel ate," I said.

"The cookies," Sin whispered. "She was eating cookies."

We all looked at him.

"What kind of cookies?" I asked.

"I don't know. They were brown with white icing."

Finnoula's mouth came open. "My molasses cookies."

Birdie nodded. "The molasses probably covers up the taste of the toxin. I sure didn't notice anything off about them."

A few things suddenly clicked in my brain, but what I was thinking couldn't possibly be true, could it? Only one way to find out.

"Finnoula," I said, "how often do you eat those cookies?"

She lifted one thin shoulder. "Almost every day."

I put my hand on George's arm. "Get your mother to a doctor immediately."

Finnoula put a hand to her chest. "You think I've been poisoned too?"

I nodded. "At the very least, you need to be checked out."

"Agreed," Larsen said. "And if there is evidence of poisoning, I need to know about it."

"Come on, Mom," George said. "Better safe than sorry." He looked at me. "Thank you, Your Highness."

"You're welcome. And don't worry about the house. I'm sure Constable Larsen can spare a deputy or two to keep an eye on things."

Larsen gave the affirmative. "We aren't done combing the house for evidence, so we're going to be here awhile anyway. I'll get some of my men working on that door too." She frowned. "Sorry about that."

George shook his head. "You were just doing your job. I'll let you know what the doctor says." Then he helped his mother out.

"Wow. Elma."

"Right?" Birdie said. "Crazy. Literally."

"I should get to work," the constable said. "I'll be in touch when I have something to share."

"Thank you. We need to go too." My head was spinning, but we had Sin's parents to prepare for. At least we could do it with the mystery of the bones behind us. And Rachel's killer in custody.

Once we returned to the palace, Birdie went to her quarters to order some snacks and work on more wedding planning. Sin and I went to see Ezreal about the impending arrival of Sin's parents just to make sure everything was set. It was, of course. Ezreal was on top of everything. Sin told him about his mother's dietary issues, then we headed back to our apartments to get ready for their arrival.

"Where exactly will they show up?" I asked. "What coordinates did my dad give you?"

"He said it was for the great hall."

"Okay, that's a good spot. Lots of space. How much time do we have?"

He looked at his phone. "Two hours." He slanted his eyes at me. "Nervous?"

"Yes. So much. I really hope they like me."

"They will, I promise." He grinned. "Should we order something sweet from the kitchen, just to settle your stomach?"

I laughed. "You know me so well."

We were twenty minutes into chocolate decadence cake with marshmallow sauce and vanilla ice cream when the apartment phone rang. Sugar and Spider, who were both lounging on the couch, looked up for a moment before deciding the phone wasn't important and going back to sleep. Such a life.

Sin made a move like he was going to get it. I put my hand on his. "You sit and relax. I've got this."

I jumped up and answered it. "Hello?"

"Good afternoon, Princess Jayne."

"Hi, Ezreal."

"Constable Larsen is here. She'd like to speak to you."

"That's fine. Send her up."

"She's on her way."

I hung up. "Larsen's on her way. I'm assuming with an update on Elma."

"Good." He wiped his mouth. "But I keep wondering what's going on with George's mother at the doctor."

I sat back down. "Me too. Today has been a crazy day, huh?"

He nodded. "And about to get crazier with my parents coming."

A few more bites of cake later, Larsen knocked at the door. Sin let her in.

"Would you like some cake?" I asked. "Or something to drink?"

"No, thanks. I don't want to take up too much of your time. Just wanted to give you an update."

"Great," Sin said. "We appreciate that. Please, have a seat."

Larsen and I moved to the couch and chairs in the sitting room, settling in around the cats, who still weren't interested in being awake.

A hint of a smile played on Larsen's mouth. "We got a full confession."

I inhaled sharply, happily shocked. "Such good news. Tell us everything." I glanced at the time. "In twenty minutes. Sorry. We've got some very special guests arriving, and we can't be late."

Larsen nodded. "No problem. Basically, Elma has been in love with George since they went to school together. When he started dating Rachel, Elma put her plan into action. But when he got engaged to Rachel, it devastated her, as you can imagine. She knew her chance to win George away from Rachel was fading fast."

"Did she actually have a chance?" I asked.

"That part seems sketchy to me," Larsen answered. "But she must have thought so. She was already working part time as a housekeeper for Mrs. Bitterbark. I guess that was her way of being as close to George as she could be. She started adding the winter primrose powder to Finnoula's tea when George and Rachel began dating. Elma knew what it would do, since her father warned her about it for years."

Sin shook his head. "Insane."

"Agreed," Larsen said. "Once Finnoula developed the symptoms of Grater's, it was easy for Elma to get hired on full time. Then, with Elma's subtle suggestions, George moved in with his mother. And Rachel, who didn't have a permanent address in the North Pole, began staying with them as well."

"And that gave Elma all the access to Rachel she needed," I said.

"It did." Larsen shook her head. "Let me fast-forward a bit now. After she used the tainted cookies to drug Rachel with the winter primrose, which definitely attacks the summer-elf system much more rapidly, she waited until Rachel passed out in her room, then Elma moved her into the unused cold-storage room in the Bitterbarks' cellar."

"How awful," I whispered. The idea of it was horrifying. "She was there all along. In the house."

Larsen nodded. "We tested the room's soundproofing. One of my deputies went in and yelled as loud as he could. The room is like a vault. Being in there…" She swallowed.

Sin looked ill. "Rachel was terrified."

"I'm sorry you had to experience that." Larsen took a deep inhale like she needed the air. "When there was nothing left but bones, Elma moved them into the Crystal Carriage. To her, the carriage represented everything she felt she'd lost out on. Love, romance, marriage. That's the same reason she framed Bonfitte. She thought having a wedding dress made by him was a dream she'd never achieve. She wanted to ruin anything connected to her broken dream."

"So sad." Sin frowned. "How did she get access to Hangar Nine?"

"George had a keycard. She stole it. I called him, and he hadn't even been aware it was gone since he never goes over there." Larsen glanced at the time. "I guess that's about it. Elma will be in holding until her trial, but I don't suppose that will be until after the wedding. No rush, really. At this point, the trial is really just a formality. After the trial, where I'm sure she'll be found guilty, we'll have to figure out what to do with her."

I nodded. "We can cross that bridge when we come to it. Any word on how Finnoula is doing?"

"Yes. Dr. Charming called with an update. It's going to take a few days in the hospital, then some close monitoring, but he believes the damage done by the years of winter primrose in her system can be completely reversed. Amazing how closely the symptoms mimic Grater's."

Sin and I both sighed at the same time. He took my hand. "That's a relief."

I nodded. "That poor family. I hope they can move on from this. George especially. He's lost so much of his life."

Larsen stood. "Time will tell. I'll be in touch if anything new develops."

Sin and I got up as well to see her out. Sin shook her hand. "Thank you for your work on this."

She smiled. "Thank your bride too. She did a lot of it. Her and Birdie."

I shrugged as Sin opened the door for her. "You know I can't keep my nose out of anything. Not when it involves those I care about."

She nodded. "It's a good quality to have. I guess I'll see you at the wedding, if not before."

"Absolutely. Thanks again." I closed the door behind her and looked at Sin. "We'd better get moving. Time to meet your folks."

His smile was tentative, but there was genuine happiness in his eyes. "Yep."

"Do you have a preference for what I wear?"

"No." He laughed. "You look good in everything. And my parents won't care if you're wearing Gucci or a burlap sack."

"A burlap sack it is, then." I put my hands on his chest, then leaned in and kissed him. "See you in the hall in ten?"

"In ten." But he caught me by the waist and held me close, suddenly serious. "I love you, Jayne."

"I love you, Sinclair." Sensing his mood, I cupped his face in my hands and stared into his eyes. "I'm going to love your parents too."

He took a breath. "I hope so."

The great hall was used primarily for royal balls. If the two adjoining galleries were opened up, the combined space could hold over a thousand people.

Usually, however, the great hall held much smaller events. Luncheons for some of my mother's charity functions. A few minor award ceremonies. And rumor had it, my great-great-great-aunt Lynette had once used this room to teach her pet reindeer, Galaxy, tricks. Supposedly, it could count by pawing the ground and prance in time to *The Christmas Waltz*. That was just a rumor, though.

Silver trim, crystal chandeliers, panels of ice-blue and white silk wallpaper, and an intricately laid tile floor in the shapes of snowflakes made the space a marvel, so it was no wonder my mother favored it for the annual royal ball.

No one who'd ever entered this room had failed to be impressed. Except, perhaps, for Aunt

Lynette's reindeer, who had allegedly nibbled off a corner of the wallpaper. But any evidence of that had long ago been repaired.

Despite the room's beauty, I found myself wondering what Sin's parents would think. They lived in Vegas, so either this room would equal the extravagance they were used to...or it would pale miserably in comparison.

My mother looked like she was wondering the same thing. She stared up at the chandeliers. "We should have had those dusted."

My father glanced at her. "We did, Klara."

"We did?"

"Yes."

"Oh." She peered at them a little longer, then frowned, shook her head, and sighed.

I'm sure the footmen by the door would carry that little tidbit into the next staff gossip session— the queen was unhappy with the job the cleaning crew had done. That ought to go over well.

Sin kept switching from hands clasped behind his back to hands in his pockets to hands at his sides.

I was chewing on my lower lip.

The only one of us who seemed perfectly at ease was my father, but then, he was Jack Frost. You didn't get much cooler. Literally and figuratively.

The air in front of us shimmered like it had gone liquid. Then two people with luggage appeared.

Sin went toward them. "Mom, Dad, you made it."

Sin's dad was a tall man with refined features and dark hair made distinctive by a widow's peak. He pulled his son into a hug. "Wouldn't have missed it for the world."

"Hi, honey." His mom smiled at him with the kind of quiet pride all mothers seemed to have around their children.

He hugged her next. "Hi, Mom. So good to see you. You look great."

"You too." She patted his chest. "It's been too long."

"I know."

She wasn't what I'd expected. In other words, she wasn't rotting away in front of us. Not going to lie, I was happy about that. She was olive-skinned, but there was a chalkiness to her skin where the glow of life should have been.

Her face wasn't traditionally beautiful, but her large eyes and strong jawline only made her more interesting. Plus, she had incredibly kind eyes and a sweet smile. I liked her instantly. And if I didn't focus on the dark hollows under those kind eyes or the ones just under her cheekbones, the shadows could have been makeup. Sort of like an overabundance of contouring and a less-than-skilled attempt at a smoky eye.

Otherwise, she was built like a Vegas showgirl, right down to her wavy brunette hair and curvy figure. There were a few places, like a patch of skin on her hand and another on the side of her neck that looked a little like they were peeling off, but I didn't care.

I wasn't going to let any of that stand in the way of getting to know the woman who was half the reason Sin had turned out so well.

Sin turned toward me, my mom, and my dad. "These are my parents, Lila and Anson Crowe. Mom and Dad, this is my fiancée, Princess Jayne Frost, and her parents, Jack and Klara. Who I probably should have introduced with their royal titles, since they are also the King and Queen of the North Pole."

My father laughed and waved his hand like he was batting those titles away. Then he stuck that hand out to Sin's father. "Please. We're going to be family. Within the confines of the palace, we'd prefer to keep things informal. Just call us Jack and Klara. And Jayne. It's our great pleasure to welcome you to our home."

Anson shook my dad's hand. "It's our pleasure to be here. We entertained the Sultan of Brunei once, but we've never met a king and queen." Then he smiled at me. "Or imagined we'd have a princess for a daughter-in-law."

I smiled back. "I'm so delighted to meet you both. And to have you here."

Lila's eyes looked a little weepy, but I wasn't

sure if that was because she was happy or a zombie. "We're so glad to meet you, Jayne."

She glanced at Sin, and the shine in her eyes changed to something easily recognizable. Joy. "I can't believe you're marrying a princess. And such a beautiful one too."

"That's very kind of you." What a sweet thing for her to say. "You know, once we're married, Sinclair will be considered a royal as well. He'll be the Prince Consort."

My mom came over as my dad and Anson were deep in conversation about what sounded like the construction of the palace. "And, Lila, you and Anson will be given the titles of lady and lord. My husband will issue a decree that makes it so. That might not mean anything in Las Vegas, but here in the North Pole, it holds some weight."

"What an honor." Lila put her hand to her throat and shook her head. "I never would have imagined the little boy who once painted the dog blue would end up with this kind of life."

I stared at Sin. "You painted the dog blue?"

He groaned. "I'd kind of forgotten about that. In my defense, I was six."

"Seven," Lila corrected.

My mom chuckled. "Considering that at the age of nine, Jayne ate half of a tray of cream tarts made especially for a visiting diplomat *before* he arrived, I think these two are well paired."

Lila laughed. "Sounds like it."

My mom smiled at Lila. "Would you like to see your rooms? Or would you rather some refreshments? We're having a family dinner tonight, so my sister and her husband—Jayne's aunt and uncle—will be joining us."

"That's wonderful." Then Lila's mouth dropped open. "You mean Santa Claus, don't you? Sinclair told us."

My mom nodded. "Yes, I do mean Santa Claus. He's my brother. We just call him Kris. He and Martha are very down-to-earth. You'll like them."

"I'm sure I will." Lila glanced over at her husband. "But I worry about Anson ending up on the Naughty List. It's hard for him to turn off the showman side of himself."

My mom snort-laughed, which caused the rest of us to crack up. She put her hand over her mouth. "Oh, he's going to fit right in. And don't worry, we don't let Kris bring the list with him to family functions."

"Good to know," Lila said. "I'd love to see the rest of the palace. Or whatever you'd like to show us."

"You're welcome to see it all," my mom said. Then she turned to one of the footmen. "Please take Mr. and Mrs. Crowe's bags up to their room."

"Yes, Your Grace." After a quick nod, he did as my mom asked.

She turned toward the men. "Jack, I'm taking Lila on a tour of the palace."

My father lifted his brows. "Oh?" He looked at Anson. "Should we join them?"

"Fine by me," Anson said. "If the rest of the place is anything like this room, I'd say we're in for a treat."

We did a quick tour of the big rooms on the first floor, then took the Crowes to their apartment on the second floor. They were close to where Sin and I were, but not so near that they wouldn't have some privacy.

We left them to get settled in. Dinner was only a couple hours away, so we'd see them soon. But Sin hesitated at the door. "Do you mind if I stay with them for a little bit? It's been a while since I saw them."

"No, of course not." I gave him a quick smile. "Spend all the time you want with your folks. I should probably go see Birdie anyway."

"Is she coming to dinner?"

My mother answered before I could. "I hope so. I'd assumed she was. I told the kitchen to prepare dinner for nine."

"I don't think I mentioned it. But she'd love that. It's kind of you to include her, Mom."

Sin shrugged. "Well, she is planning our wedding. Including her seems like the least we could do."

My mother's eyes rounded, and she turned with that kind of slow, deliberate motion that spelled trouble. "What do you mean she's planning your wedding?"

I shot Sin a look, then thought about kicking him lovingly in the shin.

He grimaced as he realized what he'd just let slip and backed into his parents' rooms. "Pretty sure I hear my mother calling me. Love you, Jayne."

He winked at me right before he closed the door. Like that was going to get him out of this.

I smiled sweetly at my mother and hoped she remembered how much I loved her. "Mom, I've been meaning to tell you. I just haven't had the chance yet, with the skeleton and everything. Birdie's helping me organize a few wedding things."

"Skeleton?" She crossed her arms. "And what kinds of things?"

My father's brows lifted. "I should get back to the office."

My mom grabbed his arm. "Just a second, Jack. Did you know about this?"

"Pretty sure I have a meeting."

"No, you don't."

He sighed. "I knew about the skeleton. But that's all been dealt with. I'll fill you in later."

If she frowned any harder, she was going to give

herself new wrinkles. "You'd better. I do not like being kept in the dark."

He kissed my mom on the cheek. "Remember, dear, it *is* Jayne's wedding."

She ignored him to look at me. "Well? What wedding things? And if you needed help, why didn't you come to Aunt Martha and me?"

"Why don't we walk and talk at the same time?" I knew my mom wouldn't like that Birdie was helping, but I wasn't going to back down.

She stayed right where she was. "Walk where?"

Wow. She was mad. "Back to my apartment. We can go see Birdie together. Fill you in on what's been happening. Please, Mom."

She frowned a little harder, something I would have thought impossible. "I suppose."

We started moving. "Look, Mom, the truth is I needed the help, and etiquette doesn't allow me to hire someone, so—"

"As I said, Aunt Martha and I are perfectly happy to step in and—"

"Three words. The wedding dress."

She sighed, and a long moment of silence followed.

I didn't want her to feel bad, but the dress had been the thing that had pushed me nearly over the wedding-prep edge. "It's not that I don't appreciate you both wanting to help, but the wedding dress is a perfect example of how that didn't really work out. You guys are too close to this whole thing. You want me to have every good thing that exists, and I love you for that, but our tastes don't always coincide."

She responded with a little indignant snort. Then, finally, words. "I guess we did interfere with that a bit."

"A bit?"

"We meant well."

"I know you did. But I had a tiny little breakdown after that whole incident."

"I'm sorry about that. We both are. Martha feels terrible about it." She shook her head. "That dress was not you. I know that. Martha knows it."

"Water under the bridge. And I'm happy to say LeRoy should have the new dress ready by tomorrow." A thought popped into my head. "I'd really like Lila to come with us when I try it on. If that would be okay with you."

She gasped. "Oh, Jayne, that's a lovely idea. Yes, absolutely. That's a marvelous way to include her."

"Thanks. I appreciate you being so open-minded about that." I was *not* going to tell her Birdie had already seen the dress.

She put her arm around me, leaning her head against mine. "Are you mad at me? About the wedding dress?"

"No!" I slipped my arm around her waist.

"Mom, I could never be mad at you about a thing like that. I was just losing it from the stress of everything. And Birdie is only here to help me not go crazy. She's great at organizing stuff like this. Plus, she's got some distance because she's not family."

"Do you feel less stressed with her help?"

"Absolutely."

"I'm glad she's here, then."

We stopped. We were at Birdie's door now. I knocked.

She answered shortly, wearing a navy-blue bedazzled velour tracksuit that really set off her blue hair. "Hello there, Jayne." Then she stopped and went into a little curtsy. "Your Grace."

"Oh, Birdie," my mom said. "You don't need to do all that. We're old friends. After everything you went through when the yetis infested your town, how could you not be dear to us?" Then she pulled Birdie into a hug. "Thank you for coming up here to help Jayne."

Birdie looked at me over my mom's shoulder, a slight hint of panic in her eyes.

"It's okay," I said. "She knows you're here to help me deal with the wedding stuff."

Birdie exhaled in relief as she and my mom separated. "I want you to know, Klara, that I'm really here for one reason only. To ease the burden on Jayne and help make this celebration something

229

she and Sinclair can really enjoy. That all of you can enjoy, really."

"Thank you." My mom meant it too. I could tell, because she took Birdie's hands in hers, something she did when she was a little overcome with feeling. "I'm afraid her aunt and I might have interfered somewhat with her wedding dress with disastrous results. So as much as I wish I could take charge of this whole wedding, I know better now. Having you here will help keep me—and Martha—on the straight and narrow."

Maybe it was the arrival of Sin's parents, maybe it was something else, but my mom was handling this remarkably well.

Birdie nodded, seemingly thinking the same thing, based on the somewhat stunned look she was giving my mom.

"Say," my mom went on, "why don't you come with us when we all go to Jayne's dress appointment tomorrow?" She looked at me. "That would be all right with you, wouldn't it, Jaynie?"

"Of course. Which reminds me…" I smiled at Birdie. "Family dinner tonight at seven, and we expect you to be there."

Birdie's mouth went into a happy little O. "That is so kind of you to include me, but if it's just family, I don't want to intrude."

"Nonsense." I knew where she was going, and I shut her down before she could get there.

"You're family. You're coming."

She smiled, a little teary-eyed. "I'm not sure I have anything appropriate to wear."

My mom smiled. "We know people. We can work that out." She gestured toward the interior of Birdie's rooms. "If I could just use the housephone?"

"Of course, I'm sorry, come in."

"Wonderful." My mom strolled through the door. "Then you can show me everything that's been planned for the wedding so far."

If my mother had any doubts about Birdie's ability to handle the wedding planning, that disappeared about three pages into the massive wedding binder she'd put together. There were sections for everything.

And I mean *everything*.

At a glance, I saw reception food, cake, drinks, wedding attire—which was subdivided into groom/groomsmen, bride, bridesmaids, flower girls, ushers, and ring bearer. There were more sections marked floral, transportation, seating chart (subdivided into ceremony and reception), time schedule, music, readings, colors, photography, video, officiant... I got a little dizzy looking at it all.

But snowballs, it was impressive.

Even my mother had gone a little googly-eyed at the level of detail. She blinked like she was trying to take it all in. "Birdie, I don't even know what to say except...wow. You are clearly the right person to handle this. I am astonished by this. And filled with a new sense of joy at what an amazing day this will be. How could it not with someone taking such careful control of it all? We are fortunate to have your help."

Birdie glowed with pride, but she shrugged like it was no big thing. "I'm happy to do it. Happy I can do it."

"So am I," I said. "Really, this is the best wedding present you could give us."

My mother clapped her hands as if she'd suddenly landed upon an idea that had to be shared. "Birdie needs something to wear to dinner this evening. I need that housephone. If you'll excuse me for a moment."

She went to make her call, leaving Birdie and me to peer at the binder.

Birdie grabbed the florist tab and pulled that section open. I stared down at a list of items on the front page as she started to read them off. "We need to get flowers confirmed pretty quickly. I talked to your florist and got a list of all the flowers the North Pole greenhouses are capable of producing. So not only do you need to decide on what kind of flowers so the florist knows if they have to be ordered, but they also need to know the kind of look you're going for, what sort of centerpieces you want, how many bouquets and boutonnieres you're going to need, and what your colors are going to be."

"First of all, the bridal attendants and grooms-men are chosen from a lottery of all the eligible young men and women in the NP. I know that probably sounds odd, but that's our tradition, and it's considered a great honor to be chosen. There are ten of each, but Sin and I won't necessarily know them."

Birdie shrugged. "Sounds fine. I'm not about to argue with tradition."

"Secondly, no outside flowers. I only want what the local greenhouses can provide. The etiquette committee wouldn't like outside flowers anyway. Not for a royal wedding."

"Right. Makes sense." Birdie made a note of that.

"I should also probably introduce you to my styling team. I'll need to bring them up to date on some of this too. Allene is my lady's maid. I really only use her when I have a special event to get ready for, but obviously, I'll need her the day of the wedding. Nesto is my hairdresser, and I haven't even begun to discuss my wedding hair with him yet. He knows what works when I have to wear a tiara, though. Same goes for Benna, my makeup artist, in that we've had no discussion about what my makeup will be that day. And then there's Davide, who handles my jewelry."

"I definitely want to meet them." Birdie flipped the binder back to the beginning and made more notes. Finally, she looked up at me again. "How about colors?"

"Sin and I talked about doing a black-and-white wedding, I guess because those colors are sort of built in already if you go the traditional route of a white wedding dress and the groom in a black tux, which we are. But now I'm wondering if we don't need a little color." I rubbed my forehead. "I promise I'll talk to him about it tonight after dinner, so how about tomorrow you and I finalize with the florist? After we see LeRoy?"

Birdie nodded. "All right. But we still have a lot of other things to finalize. Music selections. The seating chart for the reception. The list of pictures to be taken. The choice of a wedding favor. Speaking of which, the info you gave me shows you were still undecided between the carved crystal entwined rings ornament or the silver engraved snowflake ornament."

With a sigh, I collapsed onto the couch. "I really need Sin's input on some of this."

"You do, I agree, but there's a lot you can do." She sat next to me. "I know it's overwhelming, but we'll get there."

My mom finished her phone call and joined us again. "There's a rack of clothes being sent up for you to try on."

Birdie's expression was pure shock. "You just happened to have a rack of fancy clothes lying around? Palace life is a lot different than what I'm used to, that's for sure."

My mom laughed. "We don't usually, but with all the impending wedding events I need outfits for, our designers have been sending clothes daily for me to try on. Good thing we're about the same size."

"Good thing." Birdie whistled, then broke into a big smile. "So I'm going to wear a dress made for a queen?" She looked at me. "You have to take a picture of me so I can show Jack."

I grinned. She was so adorably excited by all this. "I will."

She turned to my mom. "Thank you so much for letting me borrow something of yours too. That's very generous."

"You're welcome." My mom glanced at her watch. "I have a couple things to do before dinner, so I'm going to head out, but I'll see you both in the dining room."

"I should go too," I said.

"Oh, no. Stay," Birdie said. "I want someone's opinion on what dress to wear. This is my first royal function. I want to make a good impression."

"If you want my opinion, I'm happy to give it." I sat on the couch. "See you at dinner, Mom."

"See you at dinner, honey." She gave a little wave. "See you, Birdie."

"Bye. Thanks again."

"Thank *you*."

A few minutes after my mom left, the rack of clothing arrived. The footman wheeled it into the living room, then unzipped the cover protecting the clothes and removed it. "Is there anything else I can do for you or your guest, Your Highness?"

"No, thank you. That will be all."

He left, and we immediately started pawing through the rack. Mostly dresses, but there were a few outfits with pants as well. We each picked out a handful of selections.

I held out a long cranberry number covered in spangles. "I love this, but it's too dressy for tonight."

Birdie gave it an appraising glance. "That is pretty snazzy. Say, what are you wearing to dinner this evening?"

"A little black dress with simple black heels." I pondered that for a moment. "But now I'm rethinking that. I mean, Sin's dad is a Vegas magician, and his mom is basically a showgirl. A little black dress is going to seem so boring."

"A black dress is a classic for a reason, though. And you have the kind of figure that makes simple look great."

"That's sweet of you, but I'm really wondering if I shouldn't go with more of a statement. I don't want his parents to think I'm stuffy or boring."

"They would never think that. But...how about this?" Birdie pulled out a zebra-print skirt suit. It was beautifully cut with clean lines, and the large black-and-white pattern popped.

I grinned. "That's pretty fabulous. You need to try that on."

"Don't you think it's a bit much for me?"

I snorted. "Asks the woman who dyes her hair blue."

"True." Birdie gave the suit a second look. "If I did a black shell underneath, that might be nice. Okay, I'll try it."

"What do you think about this?" I showed her the geometric-patterned sheath dress I'd just found.

She nodded. "I like that. Very modern."

"It would be great with a black jacket. Any chance you brought one with you?"

"No, but there might be one on this rack."

"Let's keep digging."

In the end, after trying on half the rack, Birdie settled on the zebra-print skirt and jacket. It was smashing on her. Not something she'd ever really worn before, but she liked to stand out, and that suit did that marvelously.

"Now," she said. "Let's go to your closet and figure out what you're going to wear."

"Sounds good to me." It was more fun than working on wedding details, although that was getting a lot easier since Birdie had arrived. Truth be told, that binder was still intimidating. Maybe just because seeing in one place everything that had to be done for the wedding made it seem like such a monumental task.

We headed to my apartment and straight to my closet.

"Oooh," Birdie cooed. "This is a great closet." Then she laughed. "Apparently, Spider thinks so too."

I turned to see. He was snoozing in a little upside-down circle on one of my cashmere sweaters. At least it was black and wouldn't show the fur. I shook my head, only pretending to be mad. "Spider, you little stinker. That's one of Mama's good sweaters."

He stretched and blinked at me without righting his head. "Spider tired. Sweater soft. Sleep good for Spider."

"Yes, I'm sure it is. But it's a shame you don't have any beds of your very own to sleep in."

"You should get him one," Birdie said.

I gave her a look. "I was being sarcastic. He has three. There's one in the living room, one in the bedroom, and one is on a kitchen chair."

She chuckled and scratched his head. "But none of those beds are cashmere, are they, little fellow?"

Spider reached out with his front feet and made a few air biscuits, then curled up tight and went back to sleep.

"Hard life," I muttered before turning back to survey the dress section of my closet. "I could wear pants, I suppose. But my mom would probably prefer me to wear a dress. It's more traditional dinner attire, even for a more relaxed event like this family function."

"What's this?" Birdie asked as she pulled out an emerald-green selection.

"That's new. I was going to wear that to the rehearsal dinner."

"It's very pretty."

"I actually have a similar dress in plum." I showed her. "But this skirt goes into pleats at the bottom."

"Oh, this is cute. I bet it's very swingy."

"It is. Might be a little too sexy for family dinner, though."

"Or not. Let me see the black dress you were going to wear."

I took that out and showed her. "I know it's simple, but I was going to pair it with some good jewelry." It had a higher neckline too.

"Hmm." She crossed one arm over her middle and leaned her elbow on it to tap a finger on her cheek. "I need to see them both on."

"Okay, no problem."

"Meanwhile, do you still have a fridge full of Dr Pepper?"

"Yes, although not the magical one from my

Nocturne Falls apartment. I had that one moved into the employee breakroom."

"That was nice of you. I'm going to get a Dr Pepper, and then I'll be in the living room." She strolled out of the closet. "You want one too?"

"Always," I called after her. I slipped into the plum dress first, pairing it with some gray snakeskin heels.

I looked at myself in the mirror. With my gray pearls, this would actually be a great look. Still a little more skin than I would typically show for a family dinner. I went out to the living room to collect my Dr Pepper and see what Birdie's reaction would be.

I did a twirl when I reached her. "What do you think?"

"That is *very* pretty." She held out a bottle of Dr Pepper to me. "What jewelry?"

I took the soda, which she'd already opened, and downed a long swallow before answering. "I have a gray pearl set that has some diamond accents."

She nodded. "With those shoes, that would be pretty hot."

"That's what I'm worried about. This is a family dinner, not a private date with Sin."

"Honey, his folks are from Las Vegas. The women dance topless there. Sometimes bottomless too. You think a V-neck is going to leave them gasping?"

"No, but that's not what this is about. Royal protocol dictates I represent myself in a certain way."

"I don't think there's anything wrong with how you look. Have you worn this dress to any functions before?"

"Once. To a cocktail party put on by the Wrapping Paper and Ribbon Curlers Association."

"And did your mother say anything to you about the dress?"

"No, but she didn't go to that event. Just my dad and I did. And no, he didn't say anything about it either. Just that I looked nice."

Birdie shrugged. "Then I say wear it. Much more impact than the black dress."

"You haven't seen the black dress on me."

"Don't need to." She sipped her Dr Pepper. "This is the winner."

"I hope you're right."

"How about this? Put this dress on, and if Sinclair makes a negative comment about it, change. If not, wear it." She sipped her Dr Pepper. "Betcha dollar the only comment he makes is how great you look."

I put my hands on my hips. "How about this bet? If he thinks it's too much cleavage, you do all the music selections for the reception, and I just have to approve them."

"Okay. And if he just says how great you look, we get the rest of these wedding decisions finalized by the end of the week."

I cringed. But stuck my hand out anyway. "Bet's on."

Sin whistled when I walked out to go to dinner. His brows shot up, too, as if the whistle wasn't enough. "Babe, you look hot."

I frowned. "Thanks a lot."

He snorted in disbelief as he walked toward me. "Um, what?"

"Sorry." I laughed. "Thank you. But you just made me lose a bet to Birdie. You look hot, too, by the way." And he did. Christmas on a cracker, what was it about a man in a dark suit with a crisp white shirt? Chillacious.

He put his hands on my hips. "What bet is that?"

I stared up at him, soaking in his handsomeness. "I thought you'd say this dress was too low-cut."

He stared at my cleavage. "What was that now?"

I giggled. "*Sinclair.*"

He winked at me. "Let me guess, Birdie thought I'd just say how smoking you are in it."

"Pretty much."

His gaze dropped again to my cleavage for a brief moment before he made eye contact. "What did you lose? Or should I ask, what did she win?"

"I have to have all of the wedding details hammered out by the end of the week."

His brows lifted again, but for a different reason this time. "Ouch. That sounds like a lot of work."

I clenched my jaw at the thought of what lay ahead. "It is."

He kissed my nose. "Hey. You're not in this alone, you know. Just tell me what I can do to help. Give me decisions to make. I'm here, ready to tackle this stuff with you."

"Okay. Thanks." I picked the easiest thing I could think of. "How about colors to start with? Are we still thinking just black and white? Because that sounds kind of boring, and I'm leaning toward throwing some color in."

He took my hands in his and stepped back like he wanted a better look at me. "What about this color? You look fantastic in it."

"Plum?"

He nodded. "I like purple."

I gave that some thought. "We could do black and white with shades of purple. I like that. What do you think?"

"I'm in. Done."

"Did we just finalize our wedding colors?" I blinked. "Is it really that easy?"

"Maybe. When you have help."

I tilted my head coyly. "Any chance you have an already prepared list of songs we can play at the reception?"

"I imagine you want the kind of songs that keep people up and dancing, maybe with a few slow ones mixed in?"

I nodded. "Yes. But they also have to be approved by the etiquette committee. So nothing naughty."

Sin smiled. "My dad loves music. In fact, he's got an antique jukebox in his man cave filled with all kinds of fun songs. We could ask him."

"Oh, I love that. Yes, let's see what he suggests. Do you have any thoughts about flowers?"

His face screwed up. "They, uh, smell nice?"

"I meant what kinds of flowers we want for the wedding."

"Oh." He shook his head. "No, sorry."

"You know what? That's okay. Just knowing what our colors are going to be will narrow down the selections." I grinned. "Hey, this isn't so bad."

"Good. And please, keep asking. I might not have answers for everything, but I can always take a shot at it."

I tugged him close. "I'm going to try on my

wedding dress tomorrow, and along with my mom, my aunt, and Birdie, I want your mom to come too. You think she'll like that?"

Sin took a breath, eyes filling with gratitude. "She'll love that. That's amazing. Thank you for including her."

"I'm happy to do it. And I mean that. I like your mom. She's very sweet. I want her to like me too."

He smiled. "She does. She thinks you're wonderful, and she's so worried about what you think of her."

I put my hand over my heart, touched by his words. "I don't want her to be worried. I really don't. I want her to feel welcome here. I want us to have a great relationship."

He cupped my face in his hands and kissed me with great tenderness. "You're a treasure, Jayne. Thank you."

He leaned in for another kiss, but a soft knock on the door broke us apart.

"I think that's my folks now," Sin said. "I told them to let us know when they were ready. I'll let them in."

I glanced at the time. "They're a little early, but that's fine. We can go down to the dining room now. Or we can sit and chat for a bit. It'll be a great chance to get to know each other."

Sin opened the door. His father stood on the other side. "Son."

"Hey, Dad. Where's Mom?"

"She's having a little wardrobe malfunction."

I walked up to them. "Hi, Mr. Crowe. Don't you look handsome! I see where Sin gets it. What's going on with Mrs. Crowe?"

He smiled. "Please, call us Anson and Lila. The buckle of her shoe broke. She's trying to fix it with a safety pin. Shouldn't be too much longer."

The poor woman. "What size does she wear?"

"I think eight?" He laughed, obviously a little embarrassed. "I should know that."

"May I go see her?"

He nodded. "Sure. You think you can fix it?"

"I think I can do better." I smiled as I went past him. I kept going until I was at their door, knocking. "Lila? It's me, Jayne."

She opened the door, one shoe in her hand, the other on her foot. Her dress was gorgeous. Royal-blue jersey hugged her body but showed no skin. I wanted to pull the neck of my dress closed. Instead, I smiled at her. "I heard you're having an issue with your shoe."

She sighed and lifted the shoe in her hand. "The buckle broke. I thought I had it fixed, but no."

I leaned in. "Anson told me you wear a size eight. Is that true?"

"I do, yes."

"Great. So do I." I tipped my head toward my apartment. "Why don't you do a little shopping in my closet to see if there's a pair in there that will work?"

Her eyes widened a bit. "That is so kind of you."

"That's what family does, right?"

She nodded, smiling. "Thank you."

"Come on, let's go see what I've got for you."

A few minutes later, Lila was wearing a pair of my heels, a strappy black number with a spray of black crystals across the front straps. "I love these. Are you sure you don't mind me borrowing them?"

"Not at all. It makes me happy that I can help. By the way, would you like to come along to my dress fitting tomorrow? My mom, my aunt, and my friend Birdie will all be there. I'd love for you to join us."

"Your wedding dress fitting?"

I nodded.

She clasped her hands in front of her. "I would adore that. Yes, absolutely I want to come. Thank you for asking me."

"Great. Now what do you say we go have some dinner?"

She nodded and off we went to get the men and then to collect Birdie.

We met everyone else in the hall just outside the dining room, where we stood around shaking hands and doing introductions. There was a kind of raucous, happy energy that didn't often come to the palace. But then, this was a family dinner, and there was a lot to be happy about. The Crowes were lovely people.

They seemed exactly like the kind of in-laws a bride would want.

We went into the dining room, but no one sat yet. Instead, the getting-to-know-you talk kept going. Mostly because the Crowes couldn't believe they were meeting Santa Claus. But also because Uncle Kris loved a good magic trick, and Anson was happy to oblige him. So much so that he made Lila disappear, which made all of us gasp, then laugh with delight when he reappeared her on the back of a unicorn.

He held one finger up to get our attention. "But watch. I'm not done yet."

At the snap of Anson's fingers, Lila dismounted with the light grace of a dancer. A second later, the unicorn disintegrated into smoke and glitter.

We all gasped again. Then we clapped, because how could we not?

"Very impressive," my father said. "Your show must be packed every night."

"We do all right," Lila said.

"Mom's just being humble." Sin's face glowed with pride. "They're booked months and months in advance."

Anson took a bow. "Thank you for allowing us to demonstrate what we do. Although in the show it's an undead dragon, not a unicorn, but I was trying to read the room."

I nodded with appreciation. "Good call."

"You know," Sin said to his father. "The family I'm about to marry into has their own kind of magic."

"Oh?" Anson's thick brows arched in interest. He looked at my dad. "How about a demonstration?"

My father shook his head. "It's not that kind of magic."

"Sure, it is," I said as I got a little shimmer, our word for our particular brand of magic, going. Soft, fat snowflakes began to fall from the ceiling.

Lila held her hands out. "How pretty. That is very cool. No pun intended. Snow is kind of rare in Vegas. We get it, but it never really lasts."

My father rubbed his hands together, and I knew he was about to show off in a way that only Jack Frost could. "We can do a little more than make it snow."

He held his hands out, and shards of crystalline-blue ice rose out of the floor where Anson had just worked his spell. The shards grew, curving and taking on a shape that suddenly became recognizable. Lila on the unicorn.

It was Anson's turn to clap. "I like that, Jack. I like that a lot. Well done, sir."

My father sketched a grateful bow, then straightened. "I'm glad you like it. But I'm not done either."

He inhaled, then blew his breath toward the sculpture. It evaporated into a cloud of ice vapor, sending a brief chill and swirls of ephemeral frost through the room that disappeared a few seconds later.

"Amazing," Lila whispered. "Can you all do that?"

"We can. To some extent," my mom answered. "But each winter elf's skill level varies. Jack is the Winter King. No one can match his ability, although our Jayne comes close."

I smiled a little self-consciously. "Comes with the territory. Uncle Kris has some pretty impressive magic too. His is mostly Christmas-related, though."

My uncle chuckled and winked at me. "We Kringles have our own skill set, that's for sure."

The chime sounded, announcing that dinner was ready, making my mother lift her chin and announce, "We should take our seats."

My father was at one end of the table, my uncle at the other, then the rest of us on the sides. I was between Lila and Birdie, who was seated next to Aunt Martha. On the opposite side, my mom sat next to my father, then Sinclair and Anson.

Dinner was served. Five courses, not including dessert. There was never a quiet moment, never a moment of contention, just a lot of smiles and laughter and storytelling.

At one point, I found myself just staring across the table at Sinclair, wondering how I had gotten so lucky and feeling utterly overwhelmed with love for him.

My heart was full. Life was good. And it was only going to get better.

"I cannot believe today is the day." I pressed my hands to my stomach, the silk of my robe cool under my fingers, but the gesture didn't do much to calm the nerves twisting my stomach into knots. Where had the months gone? How was I actually about to marry Sinclair?

My heart beat with a rhythm I didn't recognize. Everything about today seemed surreal.

Nesto, my hairdresser, smiled at me in the mirror as he smoothed my hair into a sleek, graceful style that would allow my tiara and veil to shine. "Don't be nervous. You're about to marry the man you love."

"Yes, but it's happening in front of the entire realm."

"True, but you've spoken to large crowds before. You've been in front of large crowds your entire life."

I took a breath. He was a hundred percent right. "I have been. Why am I so nervous, then?"

Benna was unpacking her makeup kit in preparation for doing my face. "Because this is personal. It's not about the crown or the throne or the kingdom. It's about you and Sinclair pledging yourself to each other for eternity. And it just so happens that it's taking place in front of the entire realm. Which is kind of like you letting all of us into your private life. That would be enough to make anyone feel a little exposed. Who wouldn't be nervous to share something so personal?"

That explanation made sense, giving me a modicum of relief. "You're both right. Thank you. That's absolutely it."

Allene was steaming my wedding dress, something she'd already done yesterday, but she'd insisted on touching it up this morning. "I think the moment you step out of the Crystal Carriage and see him waiting at the end of the aisle for you, your nerves are going to disappear. All you'll focus on is that wonderful man of yours."

"I hope you're right." I couldn't wait to see Sinclair in his tuxedo.

"She is," Davide said. He was sitting at the desk in my bedroom, a loupe on one eye, giving a final inspection to my jewelry for the day. I wasn't wearing much. Just my engagement ring, my tiara, and the diamond stud earrings that had been my graduation present from my parents. But it wouldn't do to have a loose stone or a bent prong. Not on the day that everything had to be perfect. "And when he sees you, he'll forget all his nerves as well."

I shifted suddenly, making Nesto groan. "Princess, your hair."

But I was fixated on Davide. "Sinclair is nervous? How do you know?"

Davide shrugged like he wasn't going to say more.

I understood. "I know you don't want to repeat something another staff member told you, but I want to know. I won't say a word."

Davide put down the snowflake tiara and twisted to look at me. "Will, his valet, might have mentioned Mr. Crowe was concerned that his suit wasn't pressed enough, that his cuff links weren't where he'd seen them last, and that the shine on his shoes seemed, and I quote, 'less shiny than it could be.'"

I pressed my lips together but smiled anyway. "That's sweet."

"It is," Allene said. "He's a lovely man, your Sinclair. He's mad about you."

I moved back into position so Nesto could finish my hair. For some reason, knowing Sinclair was nervous made me feel better. Like we were in this together. Which we were, obviously. But sharing

the same emotions about the day that lay ahead…
That was oddly calming. "And I'm mad about him."

An idea popped into my head. "I want to send
him a note. Bring me some paper."

Benna put down the steamer, went to my desk,
opened one of the drawers, and took out a box of
my notecards with their matching envelopes. "Will
this do?"

"Yes, perfect. And a pen."

She brought the items to me, then I hastily
scrawled a note.

*I love you and cannot wait to see you. I am so happy
to be marrying you today.*

I closed the card, tucked it into an envelope,
then sealed it. "Benna, will you take this across the
hall to him?"

"I'd be happy to, Princess." She took it from me
and left the room.

Nesto smiled at me in the mirror. "You two are
going to make the whole kingdom fall in love with
being in love."

My smiled widened. "I'm okay with that."

I closed my eyes as Nesto finished working his
magic on my hair. When he was done, Benna went
to work on my makeup. We'd decided on a bold
eye with a soft lip. I didn't want to kiss my groom
and leave him covered in lipstick.

She'd only begun to do my eyes when someone
knocked on the door.

Allene went to get it and came back with a note. She held it out to me. "I think your groom has replied."

With a smile, I tore the envelope open.

My love, all I can think about is seeing you, being with you, and becoming your husband.

P.S. Sugar insisted you say hi to Spider on her behalf.

I laughed. Spider was sleeping on the end of the bed, pretty much oblivious to everything going on. Or at least that's how he appeared.

I called his name softly. "Spider baby."

His eyes opened to little slits. I knew he hadn't been really sleeping.

I waved the note. "Sugar says hi."

His head came up. "Spider likes Sugar."

Nesto, Allene, Benna, and Davide went still. They all loved Spider and knew he could talk, but it was rare that they heard him.

"He's so cute," Benna breathed out.

Spider looked at her, then licked his foot twice. "Spider cute."

She laughed softly. "Are you ready for your mama to get married, Spider?"

Spider tilted his head. "Spider and Sugar are going in the carriage."

"That's right," I said. "You're riding in the carriage with me, then back to the palace with us after we're married. All the people will be waving to you."

He stared at me. "Spider not waving. Spider meow. Maybe."

"Oh, don't be grumpy. You get to wear a pretty purple bow tie today."

He suddenly sat up. "Bow tie make Spider look handsome?"

"Yes, very handsome."

"Okay. Sugar wear bow tie?"

"No, Sugar is wearing a purple ruffle that matches. She will look very pretty."

"Okay. Spider likes." He started to lie down, then got right back up. "Spider wants to get married too, Mama."

"You want to marry me?"

"No, Mama. Spider and Sugar get married."

"Um…are you saying you want to marry Sugar?"

"Yes, Mama."

"Okay, I'm sure we can arrange that."

"Now, Mama."

My brows lifted. "Have you even asked Sugar if she wants to marry you?"

"Sugar loves Spider."

"Okay, but—"

"Now, Mama."

"Well, Bossy Britches, hold your horses." I glanced at Allene. "Can you go back to Sinclair's and inform him of this new development?"

She nodded, barely containing her laughter. "I'm on it."

She left, returning two minutes later with Sugar in her arms. She didn't come any farther than the bedroom door. "Princess, Consort Sinclair is with me, but he's not coming into the bedroom, so he won't see you or your dress. But if you stay where you are and he stays where he is, you'll both be able to see the cats on the bed."

"Okay."

"Hi, honey," Sinclair said. "Are our cats really getting married?"

"Apparently. Love you. Thanks for being a sport."

He laughed. "Nothing surprises me anymore."

I looked at Sugar. She still had her translation collar on. "Sugar, you want to marry Spider?"

The little white cat perked up. "Sugar loves Spider. Sugar marry Spider."

"See, Mama?" Spider looked rather pleased with himself. He walked over to the bed. "Get Birdie now."

I sighed. "What made me think we could do this without her?"

"On my way," Allene said. She put Sugar on the bed next to Spider and left.

A few more minutes and she returned with Birdie.

She strode into the bedroom, a few rollers still in her hair, but she had her dress on for the wedding and her makeup done. "Is this for real? The cats are getting married?"

I nodded. "Just go with it."

"Right."

Spider and Sugar sat at the edge of the bed.

I looked at them. "Ready?"

Two meows answered me.

"Sugar, do you take Spider to be your cat husband? To love and look out for, to play with and groom, for all nine of your lives?"

"Sugar does."

"Spider, do you take Sugar to be your cat wife? To love and look out for, to play with and to groom, for all nine of your lives?"

"Spider does, Mama."

"Wonderful. With the power vested in me as heir to the Winter Throne, I now pronounce you joined in feline matrimony. You may kiss your bride, Spider."

He leaned in and nuzzled Sugar, then licked her face. She licked him right back.

All around me, my team and Birdie made little cooing noises, then started clapping. I could hear Sinclair doing the same in the other room.

I shook my head, laughing softly. "Congratulations, Spider and Sugar. I hope you're very happy together."

Birdie rolled her eyes good-naturedly. "So cute. But I'd better scram and do something about this hair."

"On that note," Sinclair said from the other

room. "I'm going to finish getting ready too. Come on, Sugar. We have to get your fancy collar on. See you at the altar, sweetheart."

Sugar jumped down and followed him out while my heart started pounding again. I nodded, which he couldn't see, then hastily added, "Yes. At the altar."

I took some deep breaths and closed my eyes as Nesto went back to work on my hair.

It wasn't long before Nesto leaned in. "I'm all done, Princess. Is there anything else I can do for you?"

I made eye contact with Nesto, then tipped my head toward Spider. "Do you think you could give someone else a little grooming?"

Nesto smiled. "I would love to."

"His brush is in the basket under the nightstand." Then I looked at Spider again. "Spider, would you like Mr. Nesto to give you a nice brushing so you look your best for Mama's wedding?"

Spider's eyes opened again. "Spider likes brushing. Mr. Nesto is nice."

I nodded at Nesto. "Thank you."

"My pleasure." He went over and got Spider's brush out, then started at the top of his head with long strokes.

Spider's eyes closed, and purrs began to vibrate out of his throat.

"Aw," Allene said. "He loves it."

I grinned. "Spider loves any attention paid to him. Don't you, baby?"

"Mama," Spider said. "Brushing time."

"Yes, I know. Don't interrupt the little prince while he's being attended to." I snorted. "Poor Sugar. Does she know what she's gotten herself into?"

Benna laughed as she turned my chair around to begin my face. "He's so sweet, though. Hard not to spoil him silly."

In between the purrs, a few more words slipped out of Spider. "Spider…likes…Benna."

With a makeup brush in hand, she touched her heart. "I like you too, Spider." Then she looked at me and mouthed the words, *I love him.*

I smiled. I totally understood. Even when he was being a little full of himself, he was adorable. I closed my eyes and let Benna get to work.

The soft sweep of her brushes against my skin and her gentle touches put me in a deep state of calm.

When I had to open my eyes a few times, I was surprised at how relaxed I really was. My nerves had faded, at least for the moment.

"Almost done," she said, brushing a little setting powder over my cheeks and chin. "There you go. Beautiful as always."

She turned me back to the mirror.

"Oh, Benna. It looks great. I look exactly how I

wanted to look. Like myself. But better. Thank you."

She curtsied. "My honor."

"You look beautiful," Allene agreed. "Now we should get you into your dress. Queen Klara and Lady Kringle are on their way with the photographer."

And just like that, my nerves were back. It was all getting very real. I got to my feet, taking a few deep breaths as I did. "They had better not make me cry, because I do not want to ruin this makeup."

"Everything is waterproof," Benna said.

I still didn't want to cry.

The door to my apartment opened, and my mother's voice rang out. "Jaynie, Aunt Martha and I are here. Where are you, sweetheart?"

"In the bedroom, Mom," I answered.

They came in, and I let out a happy gasp. "You both look so beautiful!"

They did too. Both of them were in deep shades of plum, their dresses embellished with little bits of crystal and sequins. My mom's had silver accents. My aunt's darker gown had some iridescent beads dancing across the bodice. Their hair and makeup, done by their people, were flawless.

Both of them came over to me, kissing my cheeks gently so as not to mess up my makeup.

"You're the most beautiful bride I've ever seen,"

Aunt Martha whispered with tears in her voice.

"You stop that," I said. "Do not make me cry."

My mother sniffed loudly. "She's right, though. There has never been a prettier, more elegant bride. You look like a dream."

I was getting weepy. That could *not* happen. Not this early in the day.

"We need a picture," I announced. "Where's the photographer?"

"In your living room," my mom answered.

"We'll get a picture," Aunt Martha said. "Just as soon as you put your dress on."

I looked at Allene. "Ready?"

"Just a moment, Your Highness." She took the dress off of its form and arranged the opening so I could step into it without wrinkling it. "All set."

Davide and Nesto made their way to the door. Davide gave me a quick look. "When you're ready for your jewels, I'll be back."

"Thank you." I made my way to the gown, then took off my robe and stepped into it.

Allene, with the help of my mom and aunt, fit me into it, zipping the hidden zipper, fixing the way it lay on me, straightening the skirt, and smoothing the fabric until there wasn't a single adjustment left to be made.

My mom sniffed again. "I can't believe my baby is getting married."

"Mom." My look held a gentle warning. "Please

don't make me cry. Benna worked so hard to make me look like this."

My mother smiled and nodded, but liquid edged the rims of her eyes. "I know. I can't help it." Then she laughed. "You think I'm bad, wait until your father sees you."

"Dad won't cry."

My mother, the Winter Queen, snorted. "Oh, please. That man is going to make the Meltwater River look dry."

I glanced behind them. "We should get Lila Crowe in here for a picture too."

My aunt nodded. "We should. Do you want me to go get her?"

"I can do that, Lady Kringle," Allene said. "The Crowes are in Consort Sinclair's apartment. I'll just pop over."

"Thank you, Allene." I took a look at myself in the mirror. It was staggering to see a bride looking back. Especially when that bride was me.

I took a breath, soaking in the moment. Today was the day I was marrying Sinclair. Our lives were going to change forever.

I couldn't wait.

All the pre-ceremony palace pictures were taken, my veil and tiara were on—as was the rest of my jewelry—my bouquet was in my hand, everyone was in their place, and my father awaited me at the south exit for the carriage ride to the ice cathedral. There, I would finally get to see Sinclair. And marry him.

My heart wasn't pounding so much as fluttering with anticipation, joy, nerves, and the sheer excitement of the day. I felt like I was floating, but also like I was *in* my body and at the same time somehow watching from outside it.

No single word existed that could describe what was going on inside me.

I doubted I'd ever have a day like this again. I focused on being centered, absorbing everything I was feeling, then exhaled and nodded to those around me. "I'm ready."

Two footmen held Spider and Sugar in their carriers, Allene was behind me to manage my train, and Benna was at her side with a small makeup case for any last-minute touch-ups that might be needed.

The apartment door was open, and Ezreal waited in the hall to escort me downstairs. He was in a dark suit with a blue tie patterned with the House of Frost crest. He nodded at me as I left my apartment to join him. "You are a vision, Princess."

"You're very kind, Ezreal. You look pretty handsome yourself."

He extended his arm to me. "It's my honor to escort you to the king and your carriage on this special day."

Emotion threatened to close my throat. Ezreal had been a part of my life for a long time. Having him here with me now felt right. I couldn't imagine anyone else in his place. "Thank you," I whispered.

His smile was tight, as if he was fighting emotion too. He gave me a quick nod, then lifted his chin.

I took his arm, and we began the procession to the south exit. There would be no elevator today. Instead, we took the grand staircase that led down to the palace's main entrance. All of the household staff were lined up. They bowed or curtsied as we passed. I noticed a few of the housekeepers and cooks looked weepy despite their smiles.

We made the turn and headed for the south exit. I was excited to see my father.

He was at the doors, waiting, looking very royal in his morning coat and full regalia. He wore a number of royal badges on his lapel and the sapphire and diamond House of Frost crest on a thick platinum chain around his neck. On his head was a matching platinum crown. He was every inch the Winter King.

He smiled when he saw me, then blinked hard. Was he fighting tears? Snowballs. That was something I'd never seen from him before, but then, my mom had predicted he'd cry. I couldn't believe she'd been right.

I smiled back, big and bright, my way of counterbalancing his obvious emotion and keeping myself from getting pulled under with it. "Hi, Dad."

He cleared his throat and seemed to shake off whatever he was feeling. At least on the outside. The thickness of his voice said he was still very much caught in the moment. "Hello, Jaynie."

Ezreal took my fingertips and held my hand at chest level between us. "Your Highness, may I present Her Grace, Princess Jayne."

My father took my hand. "Thank you, Ezreal."

He bowed and stepped back.

I held my smile as I glanced at Ezreal one last time. "See you at the wedding."

He grinned. "Yes."

Then my father gave me his arm. I took it, clutching my bouquet tightly in my other hand, and two footmen opened the doors ahead of us.

The carriage sparkled like it was diamond-encrusted, even in the shadows of the portico. Another footman stood beside its open door, waiting to help me in.

We left the palace, but my father paused on the outside landing. His gaze shifted to me. "You look beautiful."

"Thank you. You look very regal today. And very handsome."

"I love you, Jaynie."

"I love you too, Dad."

A hint of liquid rimmed his eyes. The emotion was back.

Something about seeing my big, strong father like this twisted everything inside me. I sniffed and took a deep breath. "If you cry, I'm going to lose it."

He laughed softly. "Hard not to on such a big day." Then he kissed my cheek. "I'm glad you're marrying such a wonderful man as Sinclair. I know I'm not losing a daughter, I'm gaining a son-in-law, but I can't help but feel that you're not going to be my little girl anymore."

Oh boy. My eyes were hot with unshed tears. "I will always be your little girl. Being married isn't going to change that, I promise."

He nodded and swallowed. "I hope not."

I patted his hand. "We should go, or Sinclair's going to think I changed my mind."

My father smiled. "Can't have that." He took a breath, and we started for the carriage. "We also can't have your mother thinking something's gone wrong. She'll be more of a wreck than she already is."

"She didn't seem like a wreck this morning when she and Aunt Martha were helping me get ready."

"She hides it well."

My entourage followed us out. One of the footmen gave me his hand to get into the carriage, then Allene helped the footmen with my train, settling it around me in such a way to keep it from getting wrinkled. Then my father got into the carriage and sat beside me. Lastly, Sugar and Spider were let out of their carriers to join us. They settled in on the top of the seat so they could see out the back.

Or in Spider's case, so he could be properly adored by the people.

The footmen bowed deeply before one of them closed the carriage door.

With a wave to everyone, we took off for the drive through town. A matched team of four reindeer in silver harnesses pulled the carriage. I squeezed my dad's hand.

We exited the palace grounds, crossed the Meltwater River Bridge, and headed into town. It didn't take us long to reach the crowds. They were lined up on both sides of the street. Some held signs and banners wishing Sin and me good luck or congratulations. Others waved North Pole flags. Some threw flowers. A few held pictures of Sin and me surrounded by hearts and wedding bells.

It was staggering to see how many people had turned out. My heart was filled by the show of love and support. I waved and smiled. Spider even lifted his paw a few times.

"I can't believe how many people there are."

My father nodded as he kept up the waving too. "This is a big day for everyone. They all want to see you."

"I hope I do them proud."

"You already have, sweetheart."

By the time the carriage entered the town square, I'd reached a place of pure calm. My father was right. The people were here for us. To support us. To share in our amazing day. I took all of that in, and then, magically, there was no room for my nerves anymore.

"We're here," I whispered to Spider and Sugar.

Spider looked up at me and gave a soft meow. I think he was as awestruck as I was at the sight spreading out before us.

The cathedral was beautiful. This was my first time seeing it complete. The arches of ice, open on the sides to keep as many views unobstructed as possible, gleamed in the bright North Pole sun.

Ivy twirled up the columns, and flowers dotted the vines, woven in amongst the green. The effect was simple, but stunning.

The carriage stopped, the footmen opened the door, and the sweet scent of the flowers flowed in. But my eyes were focused on the end of the aisle I was about to walk down.

Sin stood there looking as handsome and wonderful as I'd ever seen him. A little flutter ran through me. Not nerves this time. Concentrated joy.

My father helped me out, and the footmen arranged my train. "Ode to Winter," the traditional bridal processional, began. The light, crisp notes only added to my happiness. With my hand on my father's arm and my bouquet front and center, we started down the aisle.

I couldn't take my gaze off Sin. From his black morning coat to the plum-colored rose on his lapel, he was perfect.

Each step brought me closer to him. I was vaguely aware of all the guests. I think I was smiling and nodding at them too. But all I could really see was the handsome man I was about to marry.

A few whispers found their way to me. People telling me I looked beautiful, or congratulating me, or similar things. It was heady stuff, but I was already floating. Everything about the moment was flawless and shining with happiness.

My dad and I reached the end of the aisle. I handed off my bouquet to my first attendant, then faced my dad. He kissed my cheek, and his last whisper to me as an unmarried woman was, "I love you."

I held on to him a moment longer. My mother was visible over his shoulder. I smiled at her. "I love you both."

A single tear trickled down my mother's smiling face.

My father and I turned to face the officiant, Reverend Vandersnow. The same man who'd presided over my naming ceremony.

The reverend spoke. "Who gives this woman to be married?"

My father lifted his chin, answering proudly, "Her mother and I do."

Reverend Vandersnow looked at me. "And do you, Princess Jayne Lilibeth Frost, heir to the Winter Throne, descendant of the House of Kringle, descendant of the House of Frost, come to this marriage of your own free will, with no reservations?"

"I do."

"Then by the power vested in me by the king and queen, and with the authority of the realm, I shall marry you."

My father gave my hand to Sinclair, and the ceremony was underway.

Sinclair and I faced each other, holding hands. I wasn't sure if I was trembling or he was, probably me, but there was no denying the excitement flowing through us.

The reverend's booming voice filled the cathedral despite how open it was. "We're gathered here today as a realm to witness the marriage of Princess Jayne Lilibeth Frost and her consort, Sinclair Miller Crowe. If there is any among you who has reason this union should not go forward, speak now."

Silence followed. Thankfully, the reverend didn't let it linger long.

"We will now be led in the singing of "Blessed Day" by Wren Evergreen."

Wren was the lead soloist in the Baker's Choir, and her voice was as pure and sweet as sugar. She took the small dais prepared on the right side and began.

On the second note, the crowd around us joined in. And I did mean the crowd. Everyone inside and outside of the cathedral sang. The sound vibrated off the ice structure, echoed off the surrounding buildings, and saturated the air with the kind of music only a multitude of voices could produce.

The song was one traditionally sung at happy occasions, and while short, the sweetness of the last note lingered over us like a cool rain.

"That was nice," Sin whispered.

I answered with a very small nod and smile. Singing was a big elf thing, and there'd be a lot more of it over his lifetime, so I was glad he'd liked it.

The reverend looked at us. "Love is different for everyone. We feel it differently. We react to it differently. We process it differently. Finding someone who feels and reacts and processes it the same way you do is a difficult task. One you have both accomplished."

Soft, happy laughter lifted off the crowd.

"Now a new task lies ahead of you. The one of starting your life together. As a unit. A team. And a family. To do that, you must nurture the love that brought you together and cling to the understanding you have for each other."

Out of the corner of my eye, I caught heads nodding.

"There will be good times, and great times, and

times that try you. But it is my wish, and I am sure the wish of every citizen in attendance today, that you won't let those trying times get the best of you. Remember that you are far stronger together than you are apart."

Sin and I smiled at each other. We already knew how true that was.

"Let us now begin the vows." He turned slightly toward Sin. "Sinclair Miller Crowe, do you take this woman to love and honor for the rest of your life, promising to cherish her above all others?"

"I do." Sin spoke without taking his eyes off me.

The reverend looked at me. "Princess Jayne Lilibeth Frost, do you take this man to love and honor for the rest of your life, promising to cherish him above all others?"

I kept my gaze on Sin. "I do."

The reverend reached into his jacket and pulled out the rings. We'd put Anson in charge of delivering them. The reverend held them in one hand, lifting them up so everyone could see them. "These rings are unbroken and never-ending circles that represent the commitment this couple shares for one another. Their love for each other is as strong and enduring as these bands."

He brought the rings back down between us. "Every time you look at them, I hope you're reminded of the vows you made this day and the love you hold in your hearts for each other."

He palmed Sin's ring, pinching mine between his fingers so he could hold it out to Sinclair.

Sin released my hand to take it.

"Place the ring on her finger," the reverend directed.

I held my hand out, and Sin positioned the ring while the reverend spoke. "Repeat after me. With this ring, I thee wed."

Sinclair slipped the ring all the way on. His eyes sparkled with such happiness, I had to smile back. "With this ring, I thee wed."

The reverend gave me Sin's platinum band, and I repeated the words just as he had. "With this ring, I thee wed."

The reverend spread his hands wide and addressed the gathered crowd. "It is my great honor to pronounce Princess Jayne and Prince Consort Sinclair as husband and wife." He looked at us again. "You may now kiss the bride."

Sin pulled me into his arms, and cheers erupted, but the moment his mouth touched mine, the outside world disappeared. My husband was kissing me, and nothing else mattered.

But then a new and somewhat unexplainable sound reached our ears. Laughter. We broke the kiss to see what was causing it.

Wasn't hard to figure out. A little furry black body wearing a purple bow tie was running down the aisle toward us, meowing his head off.

The oohing and aahing and *oh, how cute*s overtook the laughter. I just stood there, shaking my head as Spider came trotting up to me.

He sat on my train and meowed up at me with great volume. I guessed he'd chosen not to speak because of the size of the crowd. Smart cat, that one. He would have caused a riot, I was sure.

I gazed down at him with a mix of amusement and love. Such a stinker. I tipped my head. "I suppose you're hungry?"

He answered with a long meow that set off a new wave of laughter.

I looked at the crowd. "My cat, everyone." I shook my head at him, then held out my arms. "Come on."

He took a giant leap and landed in them.

Sin laughed. "My wife, everyone."

That got the biggest laugh, and on that note, we headed back to the carriage with Spider acting as my bouquet. (I'd let my first attendant hang on to my real one.) The laughter turned into cheering and applause, and by the time we reached the carriage, my cheeks ached from all the smiling.

I let Spider get into the carriage on his own, where he went back to sit by Sugar. Sin helped me in, then the footmen dealt with my train again.

At last we were in and the door was closed. We had a half-hour journey home because of the slow pace and the parade route, but Sin and I were together, and that was all that mattered.

He grinned at me. "We're married."

"I know. Crazy, right?"

He kissed me. "I love you. But I'm glad that part is over."

I laughed. "Me too. That was a lot of people. And I'm used to a lot of people. But that was different."

Spider was sitting up, pawing at the carriage's crystal-clear sides.

Sin hooked his thumb toward Spider. "We should probably be waving too."

"You're right, we should." I gave him a wink. "Don't want people thinking the Prince Consort is too good for a little friendly gesture."

"No, we do not." He snorted. "I can't believe that's my title now."

I started waving. "Yep, you're stuck with being royal." I glanced over my shoulder, so in love with him that I ached with it. "You're also stuck being married to one."

He looked back at me, grabbing my hand and squeezing it. "I couldn't be happier about that."

At the end of our journey, we arrived at the main entrance to the palace. This was not the day to go in through the side entrance. And just like when I'd descended the steps with Ezreal, every available staff member had assembled to welcome us home as husband and wife.

Sin let out a low whistle. "Is that everyone who works in the palace?"

"Not everyone. There's no way the kitchen staff could be out here, not with the massive dinner they're about to put on. Plus, I'm sure there's still security at their checkpoints and a good number of valets getting ready to deal with all the vehicles that are about to arrive."

"Even so, that's a small country out there."

I nodded. "It is. Our country."

He took a breath as the carriage rolled to a gentle stop. "The footmen are going to take Spider and Sugar back to your apartment?"

"Yes, and Allene is going to take their fancy collars off them and get them fed."

"Great. I like her a lot. She's really nice. Your whole team is."

"They're wonderful. I wouldn't look like this without them. And tomorrow I'm giving them all a weeklong vacation in Vegas. Your mom helped me set it up. They're going to see your parents' show and everything."

"Hey, that's awesome."

I shrugged. "They've earned it. This wedding was a lot of work." Then I let out a little sigh. "I'm sorry we didn't manage to plan a honeymoon. I didn't anticipate how much time getting the new apartment ready was going to take. And we still won't be in for a week."

He smiled and lifted one shoulder. "We'll get to the honeymoon. We have all kinds of time.

Working on the apartment was important."

"Thanks for being so understanding."

"Of course." The door opened, and a fresh, cool breeze blew in. Sin leaned closer. "And now, after all that work, the fun part is finally here."

We had to wait behind closed doors before entering the great hall. When we did go through, Ezreal would announce us to all the guests inside.

The hall was at full capacity with both adjoining galleries opened up, which meant there were about a thousand people on the other side of the doors, waiting for us. A fraction compared to the number who'd turned out to watch the ceremony, but I also knew there were smaller versions of this party going on all over the realm this evening.

Miniature wedding cakes would be eaten in our honor. None, of course, with the particular layers of flavor that ours had, but tomorrow, White's Fine Pastries would begin production of Royal Wedding Cupcakes in the three flavors we'd chosen.

I was sure other bakeries would copy the flavors. It happened. But I didn't think any would quite match the deliciousness of what Julianne had provided for us.

"You're thinking about the cake, aren't you?"

I looked at Sin and laughed. "Do you really know me that well?"

He nodded. "Yeah, I do. Plus, you get a certain little gleam in your eye when you're thinking about sweets."

"I do?"

"Yep." He shook his head, clearly amused. "You know the cake cutting isn't for a while yet. We have to eat dinner first, have our first dance, all that stuff."

"I know. But I can't wait to eat some. After all this excitement, I could use the boost."

"I'm sure we'll find something for you once we get inside." He was grinning in such a way that I knew he was up to something.

"What?"

He shrugged one shoulder. "I might have asked the kitchen staff to have a couple bottles of Dr Pepper on ice and waiting for you at your seat on the dais."

This man. "Well, now I'm really glad I married you."

He snorted. "Is that what finally did it? Good to know."

I slid my arm around him and hugged him tight. "Today's been pretty amazing."

"It has been. And tonight's going to be a blast."

Ezreal slipped through the doors. "How are you doing? Are you ready to go in?"

We both nodded.

"Great. I'll announce you, then the footmen will open the doors." He smiled. "Here we go."

He went back into the great hall, and I could hear a microphone click on. "Ladies and gentlemen, esteemed guests of the realm, please join me in welcoming for the first time as husband and wife, Princess Jayne and Prince Consort Sinclair."

A cheer went up, and the doors opened.

We walked out, holding hands and waving. The room was lit as if twilight had fallen. Snow drifted from the ceiling in big flakes that dissolved without a trace the moment they touched our skin. The space looked like an enchanted winter wonderland. It was beautiful.

But better than that was the sea of smiling faces. There were many people I knew only in passing because they held certain offices or were the heads of organizations, but there were also many I knew and loved. Lots of folks from Nocturne Falls had come, which touched me deeply. Sin and I owed that town so much.

A happier time I couldn't imagine. The dais, where we'd be seated, also held my parents, my aunt and uncle, Sin's parents, and his great-aunt,

Zinnia, who'd come up only last night. I hadn't met her yet, but I was looking forward to it.

All of our wedding attendants were seated at the tables closest to the dais, along with the most distinguished guests. Most of the Nocturne Falls folks—like Birdie and her beau, Jack, and all my friends from the toy store—were at those tables.

As things died down a bit, we took our seats so dinner could begin. A server approached and immediately filled my goblet with Dr Pepper. I took a sip, and the sugar hit me a second later, boosting my energy.

The night progressed perfectly. Dinner, dancing, cake, more dancing, more cake. It was all wonderful. No one seemed to want to go home, either, which was fine with me. This wasn't a party that I wanted to end.

Eventually, with the first light of dawn already pinkening the horizon and our wedding breakfast only a scant couple of hours away, we left the great hall behind and headed to our respective apartments to change.

I was tired from the day, but still very much floating on a big cloud of happiness.

At my door, Sin pulled me into his arms and gave me a slow, easy kiss that lingered for a deliciously long time. I went tingly all over, and even though I was exhausted, I could just feel the bloom of fresh energy.

When he finally released me, I blinked up at him. "What was that all about?"

"Can't a man kiss his wife?"

"Definitely. Anytime he wants. Just wondering if there was more to that than opportunity."

He bent his head until our foreheads touched. "There kind of was. Mostly because we're not really going to have a wedding night until tomorrow. Not with family here and us due in the dining room for breakfast in a couple hours. Plus, I know Allene is waiting for you in your apartment just like Will is waiting for me in mine."

"True," I said. "Too bad the new place isn't done, or we could escape over there for a few hours. Next week can't come soon enough."

His right eyebrow lifted in disbelief. "You talk a big game, but I'm willing to bet you'd be asleep before I got you out of this dress."

I chuckled. "I'm not even going to argue, because today has been a long day. In fact, the only thing that's going to get me through breakfast is a shower hot enough to wake me up." I tapped one of the studs on his shirt. "Want to join me?"

A wicked spark lit his gaze. "Well, Mrs. Crowe. That's one of the best ideas you've had since we got married."

"Stick around. This marriage is young."

"Give me twenty minutes to get out of this suit?"

"Perfect. It'll take me that long to ditch this dress and get Allene out of there. Although I'm sure she'll understand."

He planted a quick kiss on my mouth. "See you then."

I backed toward my door, thankful that my train had been bustled up so that I didn't trip over it. "I'll leave it unlocked."

I went in, not only leaving the door unlocked, but partially open. "Allene? I'm ready to take this gown off."

She wasn't in the living room, which was where I'd expected her to be, so I walked into the bedroom.

I stopped at the door. Allene was frozen to my desk chair with bands of ice. Her eyes were wild and pleading. One of my scarves wrapped her mouth, gagging her. She looked petrified.

The source of that fear was right behind her. Elma. And she had Spider by the scruff of his neck. A low, guttural growl vibrated out of him. There was no sign of Sugar, but Elma had scratches on her hands.

She was going to have worse than that when I got done with her. My hands clenched in anger. "What are you doing, Elma?"

"What does it look like, Princess? Ruining your perfect day. I didn't get one, so you're not going to either."

How she'd escaped the holding cells, I had no

idea, but she was wearing the same uniform as palace kitchen staff, so it was pretty clear how she'd gotten in. If anyone wanted to slip into the palace unnoticed, today was the day. With the extra help and wedding chaos, it had to have been easy.

Obviously.

I shook my head. "You did that to yourself. And you're too late to ruin my perfect day. I've already had it. Now put my cat down and give yourself up. I'm sure the constable is looking for you."

"No one's looking for me. Not with the ice form I left under my sheets in my cell."

"That will melt soon enough." But it was obvious Elma's gift of shimmer was strong. But then, if her father worked in the stables, she had to come from a family with strong magic. That was a prerequisite for reindeer handlers. I couldn't underestimate her. "If you give yourself up, things will go easier on you."

"Easier?" She snorted. "Nothing in my life has been easy. The man I love tried to marry another woman. How could he after all I did to help his mother?"

My hands clenched a little tighter. I was not doing this. Not now. Not after the most perfect day of my life. I took a few steps toward her. "You're the reason his mother is sick. You poisoned her. And your life hasn't been easy because of the choices you've made. How about a little personal responsibility? Huh? How about that, Elma?"

"Come any closer, and someone's going to get hurt." She thrust her hand out, and an ice dagger appeared in it. With the bands on Allene, the ice form in her cell, and now this dagger, her power had to be stretched thin.

I nodded. "I agree, someone is going to get hurt, but the odds are that someone's going to be you." I called up my power and produced a long double-bladed staff of hard, winter-elf ice. I began twirling it slowly, letting the light glint off the razor-sharp edges. "I've had years of training, Elma. Do you really want to try me?"

She laughed, a rather maniacal sound. "I don't need to fight you to hurt you."

She put the blade to Spider's neck.

Every inch of me went cold, and a haze of red covered everything in my field of vision. I stopped twirling the staff. "You hurt that cat, and I will kill you. Slowly and painfully."

A second of uncertainty crossed her face, like she'd realized she'd gone too far. But it only lasted a second. Then the crazy came back. "Maybe I'm ready to die."

I needed a distraction. I looked at Spider, praying this was the one time he would talk when I wanted him to. "It's okay, baby. Mama's going to take care of this. Are you okay? *Tell* Mama you're okay."

He looked at me, eyes narrowed. Then they went wide with understanding.

"Not okay," Spider said. "Bad lady hurting Spider."

Elma's mouth dropped open, and she looked down at Spider. "What the—"

I dropped the blade and thrust my hands at her, freezing a solid block of ice around her head. At the same time, Spider bit her.

With a muffled howl, she dropped Spider and the dagger, putting her hands to the ice. Spider ran off as I added another layer of ice to Elma's headgear, freezing her hands in place at her ears.

"I told you not to try me."

The weight of the ice was too much. She toppled over and sprawled on the carpet, kicking her legs in a feeble attempt to break loose. As she used up her oxygen, the kicking weakened. She'd die if I left her like that. I couldn't have that. She needed to answer for what she'd done, and I would not be responsible for her death.

Being trapped like that was taking her focus off the rest of her magic, though. The bands around Allene were melting away.

"You okay?"

She nodded, no longer looking panicked, but her gaze was on Elma. Allene grunted something I couldn't make out, jerking her head at the flailing woman.

I looked over. Elma had the ice block partially defrosted already. She was skilled, that was for sure.

Sin came running in with Spider at his heels. "What's going on? Spider said there's a bad lady—*whoa*."

"Yeah," I said. "Will you help Allene?"

"On it."

I stood over Elma with my hands outstretched, reabsorbing the cold to release her from the ice. "Is Spider okay?" I asked Sin without looking away.

"He seems to be. Was he in danger?"

Allene's scratchy, "Thank you," told me Sin had gotten the gag off of her.

"Yes."

Elma was out of the ice. She gasped, refilling her lungs, hands at her throat.

I wasn't waiting. I grabbed her and hauled her to her feet. "This one had a dagger to his neck."

Elma raised her hands like she was about to fight.

I glared at her, daring her with my eyes to do something stupid. "Did you really enjoy not breathing so much that you want to go back into that block of ice?"

She scowled but dropped her arms to her sides. "I hope you get divorced."

Sin brought the scarf over that had been around Allene and bound Elma's hands with it. "That's not going to happen. Not ever." He looked at me. "What's the jail time for breaking into the palace, tying up a member of the royal staff, and threatening a royal pet?"

"More years than I can count. Which reminds me, I haven't seen Sugar."

Spider leaned his front paws on my dress. "Sugar in the closet, Mama."

I nodded at Spider. "Is she all right?"

"Sugar sleeping."

"Maybe you should go check on her."

"Okay." Spider trotted off in that direction to check on his furry little wife.

Allene was on her feet now. "I'll go call security."

"And the constable, if you can raise her."

She nodded. "Will do."

She slipped out of the room, leaving us with Elma. We had her between us, each with a grip on one of her arms.

Sin frowned. "I feel sorry for you, Elma. You could have had love. A happy life. A family of your own. But you were too filled with hate to make room for it."

She snarled at him. "Save your platitudes, necromancer."

He shrugged, clearly amused. "Suit yourself. I'm not the one headed back to a holding cell, though."

I grinned at him. "Nope. You're headed to the shower."

His response was a wide, immediate smile. "Still on for that, are we?"

Elma looked about ready to throw up, which only tickled me more.

I nodded. "Who cares if we're late for breakfast?"

Elma made gagging sounds.

Sin laughed. "Not me."

Before we could get into that shower, we had to turn Elma over to the constable. Fortunately, after Allene called security and the word went out about what had happened, the constable was quickly tracked down at her house. Just arriving home, I might add. Larsen had stayed at the reception longer than my parents, who'd left about an hour before we had.

Within twenty minutes, Larsen, Ezreal, Rizzle, head of palace security, my father, and Sin's parents were in my apartment.

It was loud and crowded and didn't feel like Sin and I were about to get any alone time soon. We looked at each other and shrugged. Not much we could do about it at this point.

"My apologies, Your Highness," Larsen said to my father as I approached. "I don't know how she escaped, but she must have been planning it for a while so she could time it with the wedding."

My father nodded. "I hate to think it was a flaw in the design, since I approved those plans." He sighed. "Thankfully, no lasting harm was done. But the next time we have a royal event, we'll have to do a better job of watching who comes in through the kitchen."

I stood at my father's right. "But how would she have gotten hold of a kitchen uniform? She was locked up."

Ezreal walked over. "I can answer that. We found one of the kitchen workers knocked out and dressed in a jail uniform behind a snowdrift near the kitchen entrance. She was Elma's size. Had quite a goose egg on her head."

Poor woman. "So Elma waited for someone her size to come out, then clobbered her and took her clothes."

He nodded. "Looks that way."

Larsen went to hitch up her utility belt, but since she was still in the sparkly navy pantsuit she'd worn to the wedding, she ended up empty-handed. She smoothed down her jacket instead. "That'll add to her charges. I'll need to speak to that worker."

"Sure," Ezreal said. "I had one of the valets take her to the hospital for a checkup, but I imagine she'll be back in a few hours, provided there's no serious injury. Either way, I'll make sure you have all her contact information."

"Thank you." Larsen looked at me. "Are you okay, Princess?"

"I am. She had a dagger to my cat, though. That has to be some kind of crime. Threatening the life of a defenseless animal."

Larsen, to her credit, maintained her serious expression. "I'll come up with something."

My father crossed his arms. "Speaking of coming up with something, what are you going to do to make sure Elma doesn't escape again?"

Larsen frowned. "For one thing, we're going to keep her under constant surveillance. For another, I have two of my deputies going over her cell right now to figure out how she escaped. Fortunately, we have two other cells we can keep her in. Once we know they can't be breached in the same way, we'll secure her in one of those. But obviously, keeping a better watch on her is paramount."

I looked at my dad. "What are we going to do with her once she's sentenced? Because she's clearly guilty. She confessed."

He uncrossed his arms. "After what happened with Gregory, your uncle and I had plans drawn up for a detention center. When Elma was arrested, we gave the green light for the facility to be built. We didn't tell you about it because you had enough on your plate with the wedding. It'll be a few more months before the CDC is complete, but then Elma will be sent there. We'll probably send Gregory out there too."

"The CDC?" I asked.

Larsen nodded. "The Coldwater Detention Center. It's a desolate place at the outer edge of the polar forest. Yeti country. But that's part of the deterrent."

I grimaced.

Larsen shot me a look. "She's a murderer, Princess."

"I know. It's where she deserves to be. Still, not an easy thing to think about." Had marriage made me softhearted? Maybe. Or maybe I was just riding the high of so much wedding bliss.

"I suppose not," Larsen said. "But we can't exactly put her under house arrest like we did with Gregory."

"No," my father said. "Not with someone who's taken a life. And really, he tried to. He needs to be there too."

Sin's parents were leaving, so he came over to us.

"Everything all right?" I asked.

"Yes. They just heard all the commotion because their room is so close. Wanted to make sure we were okay."

"Of course." We'd put them in the same room they'd stayed in the first time they'd come up.

"I asked them to go to my apartment and check on the cats."

"Is that where they went?"

Sin nodded. "Last I saw, Spider and Sugar were on the bed."

"At least they're getting to enjoy some post-nuptial alone time."

Sin laughed.

Larsen cleared her throat. "If you don't need me for anything else, I should go. The deputies will have her at the station by now, and I plan to do a full interrogation."

"Thank you, Constable," my father said. "Let us know what you find out."

"I'll have a copy of my report on your desk as soon as it's finished." She gave us a nod, then left.

The remaining deputies went with her.

Ezreal gave us a short bow. "I should go as well."

My father nodded. "That's fine, I know you have a lot to do, but please, do the minimum, then take the rest of the day off. We've all been going nonstop for a while now. You need the rest as much as I do."

"But I have—"

"Whatever it is, it can wait," my father interrupted. "The minimum, Ezreal."

He smiled. "Yes, sir." With a quick nod to Sin and me, he left.

My father turned to us. "I'm going too. I need to explain to your mother what's happened, although she might already be in the dining room making sure everything is underway for breakfast."

I checked the time. "Snowballs. Breakfast is in less than forty-five minutes."

"Do you want to cancel it?" my father asked.

"No." But I looked at Sin all the same. "Do you?"

"No." He hesitated, a mischievous smile bending his mouth. "After all, we leave for our honeymoon tomorrow. We can certainly spend this time with family."

I stared at him for a moment. "We decided to postpone our honeymoon because we didn't have time to plan it properly."

Sin's smile expanded. "Did we, though?"

My father held his hands up in surrender and backed away. "See you at breakfast."

"Okay." I nodded, but I was still fixated on Sin. "What aren't you telling me?"

"With Birdie's and my mom's help, I got the honeymoon taken care of. We leave tomorrow. We're doing a five-day Alaskan cruise, then a week in Vegas with my parents—we'll be in their guesthouse, so plenty of privacy—then on to Hawaii for another week. What do you think?"

My mouth was hanging open, but I didn't care. I let his words process before answering, which took a few seconds. "You did all that?"

He nodded, looking very pleased with himself.

But then, he had every right. He'd really surprised me. "Is that okay?"

"Okay? It's wonderful. Wow! And I am so glad you did it. I can't wait to spend three weeks with you just being a newlywed couple." I hugged him. "Thank you."

He pulled me in tight. "I just want to make you happy for the rest of our lives."

"I don't think you're going to have any problem doing that." I leaned back. "There's just one thing. What about the cats? I mean, I know the staff can take care of them, but—"

"Birdie's going to babysit. It's all taken care of."

I exhaled and leaned my head against his chest again. "You really are the man for me."

He chuckled softly. "Good thing, considering we just made it official. I love you, Mrs. Crowe."

"I love you too, Prince Consort."

He kissed the top of my head. "Now let's go get some pancakes."

The End

Want to be up to date on new books, audiobooks & other fun stuff from Kristen Painter? Sign-up for my newsletter on my website. No spam, just news (sales, freebies, releases, you know, all that jazz).

www.kristenpainter.com

If you loved the book and want to help the series grow, tell a friend about the book and take time to leave a review!

Other Books by Kristen Painter

COZY MYSTERY

Jayne Frost series

Miss Frost Solves a Cold Case: A Nocturne Falls Mystery
Miss Frost Ices the Imp: A Nocturne Falls Mystery
Miss Frost Saves the Sandman: A Nocturne Falls Mystery
Miss Frost Cracks a Caper: A Nocturne Falls Mystery
When Birdie Babysat Spider: A Jayne Frost Short
Miss Frost Braves the Blizzard: A Nocturne Falls Mystery
Miss Frost Chills the Cheater: A Nocturne Falls Mystery
Miss Frost Says I Do: A Nocturne Falls Mystery

Happily Everlasting series
Witchful Thinking

PARANORMAL ROMANCE

Nocturne Falls series
The Vampire's Mail Order Bride
The Werewolf Meets His Match
The Gargoyle Gets His Girl
The Professor Woos The Witch
The Witch's Halloween Hero – short story
The Werewolf's Christmas Wish – short story
The Vampire's Fake Fiancée
The Vampire's Valentine Surprise – short story
The Shifter Romances the Writer
The Vampire's True Love Trials – short story

The Vampire's Accidental Wife
The Reaper Rescues the Genie
The Detective Wins the Witch
The Vampire's Priceless Treasure

Sin City Collectors series

Queen of Hearts
Dead Man's Hand
Double or Nothing

STAND-ALONE PARANORMAL ROMANCE

Dark Kiss of the Reaper
Heart of Fire
Recipe for Magic
Miss Bramble and the Leviathan

URBAN FANTASY

The House of Comarré series:

Forbidden Blood
Blood Rights
Flesh and Blood
Bad Blood
Out For Blood
Last Blood

Crescent City series:

House of the Rising Sun
City of Eternal Night
Garden of Dreams and Desires

Nothing is completed without an amazing team.

Many thanks to:

Cover design: Keri Knutson
Interior formatting: Author E.M.S.
Editor: Joyce Lamb
Copyedits/proofs: Marlene Engel

About the Author

USA Today Best Selling Author **Kristen Painter** is a little obsessed with cats, books, chocolate, and shoes. It's a healthy mix. She loves to entertain her readers with interesting twists and unforgettable characters. She currently writes two best-selling paranormal romance series: Nocturne Falls and Shadowvale. She also writes the spin off cozy mystery series, Jayne Frost. The former college English teacher can often be found all over social media where she loves to interact with readers.

www.kristenpainter.com

Made in the USA
Middletown, DE
07 January 2020